NIGHTWALKER 5

NIGHTWALKER 5

WRITTEN BY CRAIG MARTELLE, CREATED BY

FRANK RODERUS

LMBPN

DISRUPTIVE IMAGINATION

NIGHTWALKER 5 TEAM

Thanks to my Beta Readers

Micky Cocker, Dr. Jim Caplan, Kelly O'Donnell, and John
Ashmore

Editor
Lynne Stiegler

CHAPTER ONE

Wolfe shouldered his AR-15 and watched for movement in the distance. The young girl, Jennifer, was curled up with the big German Shepherd-wolf mix, Buddy. The two were inseparable and reminded him every day what he was fighting for.

The nuclear holocaust had caught Wolfe in Idaho, thousands of miles from his home and—far more importantly—his family in Bradenton, Florida. The bombs had shattered the United States, creating hot zones, red zones flooded with harmful radiation, and clear areas where no radiation remained. To escape the fallout from the bombs that had targeted Boise, Wolfe had holed up inside an old mine shaft. Subsisting on the foods that were in the long-haul truck he had been driving, he had stayed there for more than two years until he was out.

Somehow, due to radiation or strange chemical components in the water that seeped out of the walls, he had become immensely strong and quick. His hair had turned white, and his beard no longer grew. He could also sense radiation as a tingle in his fingertips. That came in handy to keep him safe in the Hot Zone. The biggest change, however, was his eyesight.

When he emerged, he had found himself unable to see in the daylight. Darkness was his new friend. He did not know how or why those things had happened to him. He simply accepted them for what they were. He found welding goggles, and wore them most of the time to keep away the searing pain of the sun's rays.

James Wolfe had been greatly changed by the time he spent in that mine, but none of that mattered to him. All he cared about now was to get home to Lurleen and their toddler JoJo—Joseph Henry Wolfe IV, named for Wolfe's father and grandfather.

Home to his family, if he could find them.

Home to his family, if they still lived.

There was one hitch. Wolfe had run afoul of some brothers, smugglers who scavenged manufactured goods from the radioactive Hot Zones. The Alston brothers had accused him of murder, and now Wolfe was a fugitive in the Clear Areas, the zones governed by a new entity called the Federal Command.

Darkness had fallen a few hours prior, and Wolfe wanted to cross into the Clear Area, away from the checkpoints, away from the criminal looks of the FEDCOM soldiers. They were no better than the wilders on the other side of the meandering border, the ill-defined separation between two areas. Both were unsafe, but for different reasons.

Wolfe broke down the AR-15, separating the upper and lower receiver groups, and wedged them into his pack. When he was in the Clear Area, he didn't want to stand out. The other times he'd had the displeasure of dealing with FEDCOM, only the soldiers had been carrying military-style rifles. At least openly. Wolfe had his bow and blowgun. He also had camp gear, a sleeping bag, and a few items of clothing. It was more than most had, and a treasure to be cherished, or something to be coveted by others.

His gear had been taken before, more than once, but he had always gotten it back. He vowed to not let anyone take what was his. The welding goggles hung around his neck, a permanent attachment to his body. He could not function without them, not in polite society that lived and worked during the daytime. The wilders had tried to take that away from him.

"I let the Alstons live, and that has caused me too many problems," he muttered. "No more. If you cross me and mine, you have taken a step toward your personal abyss. The only way to defeat scum like you is to beat you back into the Stone Age."

Wolfe's knuckles turned white from the fists he clenched. He stared into the darkness, wondering if he would encounter them again or if he was free of their malicious influence.

Jennifer stirred, blinking into the darkness. "Mister Wolfe?"

"I'm right here, Miss Jennifer."

"I overslept. I'm sorry," she started, but he stopped her when he picked up her small pack and handed it over.

"Nothing to be sorry for. When you're ready, we'll cross into the Clear Area. Should be easy walking for you and Buddy."

He could see her nod in the darkness, but she could not see his smile. Buddy trotted away to take care of business. A minute later, there was a scuffle in the brush. Wolfe ran that way until he came across the dog carrying a dead rabbit in its mouth.

"Go ahead and eat, dog." Wolfe returned to the young girl and sat down with her. "What do you want to be when you grow up?"

"What is there?" she asked.

He had told JoJo that he could be whatever he wanted to be. That was no longer true. "I guess, Miss Jennifer, we are going to have to find out by seeing for ourselves. None of that," he waved his hand at the world behind them before shifting to point at the way ahead, "and all of that."

In the distance, random lights flickered from those blessed with power. They lived in the Clear Area. Blessed was probably the wrong word, but they were doing what they had to do. Wolfe hoped they had a public transportation system of some sort. The girl was keeping up without complaint, but walking all two thousand miles would take its toll. He would protect her, but was it the right way to raise her?

He struggled with the answer.

Buddy returned, tail wagging while his tongue worked overtime cleaning his muzzle. Jennifer patted his head, and the three started walking.

CHAPTER TWO

Jennifer kept her head down, as did Jim Wolfe. Daylight had come, and with it, the three found themselves almost ten miles inside the Clear Area. Normal people outnumbered the soldiers on the outskirts of a town that threatened to turn into a city. A river flowed from the north. Wolfe wondered if it was the same one they had followed out of Canon City before turning south.

The Arkansas River. He had almost forgotten the name. Did people remember what things were called, or were they giving rivers and mountains new names? Paradise. Not paradise at all, but the name had changed. A new opportunity for people with ambition. A new opportunity for bullies to run wild. Maybe that was where the name "wilders" came from.

It was going on three years since the bombs had fallen. Three long and painful years. Wolfe clutched the bow he carried over his shoulder while his other hand swung free. He tried to look casual but was tense as a horse that smelled blood. Or one that saw a rattlesnake coiled on the trail ahead, head up and tail rattling.

His fingertips didn't tingle, and that was something. They would not have called it the Clear Area if there was radioactivity burning holes through the people. At least the air and land were safe, although Wolfe could not speak for anything else. In his travels, he had found that Clear Areas were as dangerous as Red Zones.

"Excuse me," Jennifer said to an older woman who was approaching them on the sidewalk. Wolfe was shocked and gritted his teeth. He expected her to scream for the soldiers to protect herself from the strangers. "Where might we get a drink of water?"

The woman eyed Wolfe cautiously. He hoped his brown-dyed hair would make him look different from any posters with his description if the Alstons' influence had made it this far south and east.

"Yes, dearie. You look like you could use a bath, too. You'll want the boardinghouse up ahead. They'll take care of you and your..." she searched for the word, "father?"

"My Pa and I only want a drink and then to be on our way."

The older woman took a knee before producing a handkerchief from the folds of her skirt. She licked at one corner and used it to clean Jennifer's face. The young girl stood still during the attention.

"Stop by the boardinghouse. Tell them Bessie sent you, and that I'll be there shortly."

She stood and gave Wolfe a full once-over before reaching for his goggles. Wolfe caught her hand with a motion too quick for the eyes to follow. He immediately let go, keeping his hand up and holding it to the side. "I have a problem with my eyesight," Wolfe said softly. "These glasses hold most of the pain at bay. My eyes are brown if you were wondering, but they don't work exactly right. Miss Jennifer and Buddy make sure I get where we need to go."

The older woman nodded knowingly and lowered her hand.

"My apologies, mister. Go to the boardinghouse. I'll join you in two shakes of a lamb's tail."

Wolfe and Jennifer watched her go. "I've had bad luck with boardinghouses that catered to strangers." Wolfe was torn. The girl needed a bath. He remembered his last hot shower—at a boardinghouse, just before he went to war with the hosts.

Buddy didn't seem to care. Jennifer was happy, and that made the big dog happy. Wolfe hung his head for a moment.

"I'll watch your back, and you watch mine," Jennifer told him. She deserved a better life, but this was the best Wolfe could do. Wasn't that what family did? Watch each other's backs? That made life safer and worth living.

The houses were scattered along the before-time streets. The garages and sheds had been turned into places of work. Wolfe couldn't see what the people were doing, but they were laboring away inside. He looked this way and that, trying to see in, but couldn't, and worried that he was being too obvious.

"I'll go look, Mister Wolfe. Nobody will worry about me."

He was torn about letting the girl go by herself but saw no other way. He was trying to avoid going to the boarding-house for as long as possible.

"Take Buddy with you, and stay where I can see you. If you yell for me, I will be there before you hear the last echo," he promised.

"I know you will. If anyone tries to hurt me, I think the only yell you'll hear will be theirs when Buddy lets them have it. He's a good dog, and I love him."

Wolfe's lip twitched into a smile, the kind he saved for those he cared about.

"Off you go, now." He leaned against a tree growing

between the sidewalk and the street. No cars remained. Whether they had been driven away or removed after the war, he would never know. He did not care enough to find out. It simply was, and he accepted it.

Jennifer skipped as she walked, her hand caught up in the German Shepherd's scruff. They reached a garage, stopped, and stood patiently watching. Someone inside flicked a hand to shoo them away. Jennifer curtsied politely and walked casually to a shed next door, where a woman walked out to greet her and pet the dog.

Buddy. Wolfe listened, looked, and scoured his memory. There were no dogs in this town, which made Wolfe and Jennifer stand out. He had taken great pains to fit in, dying his hair, hiding his rifle, and walking with a family. But the dog… Like Jennifer, he would not leave either behind.

The woman reached for the girl and grabbed her. Wolfe took a step forward, but it was just a hug. They waved, and the woman went back into the shed. Jennifer skipped her way back.

"They are making replacement parts for the electrical system," she said, enunciating the words as if she'd memorized them.

"Why did those men chase you away from the garage?"

"They were grinding something, and sparks were flying out the door. They yelled at me to be careful, and keep Buddy out of the way, too."

"Makes sense," Wolfe conceded. "And the woman?"

"She was nice." Jennifer did not say anything else about the shed or the woman's explanation of what they were doing.

"Why wouldn't they use a larger machine shop instead of hobby tools in garages?" Wolfe wondered. Jennifer shrugged and ran into a yard to make Buddy chase her. The two played as Wolfe herded them in the general direction of the board-inghouse.

"Maybe things are more normal the farther one gets into a Clear Area," Wolfe mumbled. But the people here earning his trust? That took something completely different.

CHAPTER THREE

"What can I do you for?" The man was dressed in dirty bib overalls and a stained and torn t-shirt. His hair probably had not been cut since the war. Or his fingernails for that matter, but his smile was genuine, and in Wolfe's book, that mattered more than a bath.

"Bessie sent us. We were looking for a drink of water and maybe to refill our canteens while we are here. Then we will be on our way. Much obliged for any kindness you can show us."

"Sure. Sink over there works, but not the toilet. They don't have the sewage system up and running yet, but they promise it will be soon. Where'd y'all come from?"

Wolfe could not lie. He believed people deserved the truth, or as much as there was to tell, but no more. "Hot Zone to the west and north of here. We were able to detect the radiation, so we stayed clear of anything harmful."

"Like a Geiger counter? Those will save your life, but no need for those here."

"Something like a Geiger counter, yes. It is nice to be in a place that is safe." Wolfe squinted through his goggles, knowing the man could not see his eyes.

"Nice dog. Can I pet him?" the man asked.

Jennifer didn't have to do anything. Buddy worked his way around the back of the counter. The man dropped his hand but then started to yell. The dog shot out from behind the counter, stopping halfway across the open area that used to be a living room to eat the sandwich he'd stolen. The man's shoulders hunched after the first step.

"It's been a while since I seen a dog. I should have known. They don't like us eatin' in front of the customers or my sammich woulda been out of reach."

"I'm sorry, mister," Jennifer said. "But I don't think there's anywhere you could have put your sandwich that he would not have gotten it."

The man chuckled.

"How can I make up for that?" Wolfe asked, looking angrily at the dog. Buddy was as happy as could be until he realized he was being glared at by all the humans in the room. His tail dropped, and he slunk over to a couch before jumping onto it and licking his front paw while looking with puppy-dog eyes at those who watched him.

Wolfe pulled off his pack and reached into it, pulling out a can of beans. Supplies like canned food were hard to come by. He didn't want to give them up, but the man looked like he only had one chance to eat, and Wolfe was not going to be responsible for his lack of food.

"Take it." Wolfe put it on the counter. "I thank you for letting us have some water."

Wolfe nodded toward the bathroom. Jennifer hurried over, taking the two canteens from Wolfe, in addition to her own.

The can sat on the counter, neither looking at it as they stood in uncomfortable silence.

"Was that a rifle you had in your backpack?"

Wolfe stood a little taller, his mouth set. "The Hot Zones are dangerous. Sometimes a bow is not the right tool for the job. I also have a blowgun." Wolfe showed the man the tube and one of the pellets.

"That works? On what?"

"Birds, rabbits. Not squirrels. Those things are tougher than shoe leather," Wolfe quipped.

"And the bow?"

"Deer, wild boar. Antelope if I can get close enough."

"The rifle?" the man pressed in a low voice.

"Elk. And that mountain lion pelt she wears." Wolfe nodded toward the bathroom. He didn't want to add that too many times, men had been in his sights. The deadliest creature of all.

"That much game is in the Hot Zones? I heard it'll melt your face off out there."

Wolfe laughed.

"My eyes were hurt in the wilds, but we still have our faces. Buddy eats well enough, but still loves a good sandwich."

"How long you been out in the Hot Zone?"

"Three years," Wolfe answered honestly. Jennifer finished, and Wolfe stuffed the two canteens back into his pack, cinched it tight, and nodded to the man behind the counter. "A pleasure."

"I'd like to hear more," the man said.

Wolfe wondered how much longer the man would try to keep them there. He felt like he was stalling. He had no interest in learning the man's name. He only wanted to leave.

"We need to go. Thank you."

Wolfe ignored the man's protests while Jennifer called to the dog, who vaulted halfway across the room to join the pair walking out the front door. Wolfe glanced through the front window before opening the door. Bessie was reaching for the handle.

CHAPTER FOUR

Wolfe stepped back, pulling Jennifer with him. Bessie opened the door and walked into Buddy, who was ready to be outside. He was okay with being indoors, but he preferred being outside. He sniffed her while wagging his tail vigorously.

"Aren't you going to stay?" the older woman asked. It was not really a question, more of a statement. She remained in the doorway, blocking their exit. The impasse continued since Wolfe didn't want to hurt her. He kept glancing out the window, looking for a truck filled with FEDCOM soldiers to come after them. "What are you looking for?"

Wolfe didn't answer.

"You think I turned you in to the Feds?"

Wolfe figured he'd better speak if he wanted a chance out of this mess before he was forced to start hurting people. "What would you turn us in for? We are traveling through on our way home. It is finally safe enough that a man and his daughter can keep from getting killed. It wasn't always that way."

"It's the opposite, Mister. You need us to protect you from the Feds. There are two worlds here…"

"Hey!" the man behind the counter protested. He pounded his fist next to the can of beans that remained where Wolfe had put it.

"Hush yourself, Gemini. I know a warrior when I see one, and this one ain't too fond of FEDCOM."

"He's hidin' a rifle in his pack," the man called Gemini offered. Wolfe looked back and forth between the two. He pulled Jennifer close in case he needed to pick her up and carry her while they made a break for freedom.

"I told you I could tell. I figured that." She waved her hand at Gemini to be quiet.

"I'm not a soldier. Far from it. I don't want to fight. I just want to get back home to my family. I'd take it as a kindness if you let me go."

Her expression softened as she held up her hands. "I think you have the wrong impression of me. By telling you what I'm about to tell you, I'm risking my life, but I'm a good judge of character, and you are the kind of man we need on our side. Desperately."

Wolfe stopped her with a single hard look. "Then maybe you should not tell us anything and let us go on our way. We want to leave in peace."

Bessie ignored him and started to talk. "We have an underground movement to free ourselves from the hellspawn called FEDCOM. Their soldiers are devils. No woman is safe. Families are an inconvenience. They are the masters, and we are the servants. They live well, and we survive.

Wolfe looked back at the can of beans on the counter. A sandwich, the man's only meal. Wolfe started to reconsider but caught himself. "I'm not a soldier."

"You are more of a soldier than anyone we have. I'm not. Gemini there isn't. The other hundred members aren't."

"You have one hundred members and have not yet been found out?" Wolfe shook his head. "FEDCOM has eyes and ears everywhere. Snitches. Turncoats. The refuse humanity has thrown away is given a uniform and power. I cannot tell you how much I have grown to despise those criminals and thugs who order people around worse than cattle."

Bessie finally moved away from the door. She *was* a good judge of character, since that was the point when Wolfe and Jennifer had decided not to flee. They would hear her out.

"We lost a bunch in the beginning. Taken away in the middle of the night at first. They were never afraid, but at least they tried to make believe they were the good guys. They turned to taking people in the middle of the day, made examples of 'em. It drove us farther underground, but we grew. With each abuse, we added members. With you, we can turn the tide, take them in the middle of the night. You see just fine in the dark, don't you, Mister Wolfe?"

Wolfe winced and Jennifer gripped his hand more tightly.

Bessie pulled a piece of paper from a pouch in her apron. It was the wanted poster with Wolfe's likeness, complete with the welding goggles.

"Dying your hair can only go so far. FEDCOM ain't stupid."

"I can't go without the goggles. Not in the daytime."

"I figured," Bessie replied. "We are about to own the night, thanks to you. It's time to strike back for all the decent people."

"I'm not a soldier," Wolfe repeated weakly.

"You're the best soldier we got, Mister Wolfe."

"You can call me Jim. This is Jennifer, and the shaggy beast is Buddy. Before we go any further, we need to get a few things straight…"

CHAPTER FIVE

The back office of the boardinghouse was kept in good order. Bessie probably would not have it any other way. It was the office, but also the kitchen. Meals did not come with boarding unless you were James Wolfe and Jennifer. Then you were someone to be wined and dined.

Even if you weren't a soldier.

Wolfe reluctantly joined Bessie in her conversation about the underground by listening to what she had to say. Gemini stayed out front where he could keep watch.

The first thing Bessie did was show Jim and Jennifer the secret way out.

"Under this rug is a trap door." She pulled the rug aside, then unlatched a recessed ring and pulled. The door opened to show steps heading into the darkness. He cupped his hands around his face and pulled his welding goggles free. There was a landing at the bottom. To the left was the basement, positioned under the main house. To the right was a passage leading away. "Take that passage and you'll end up on the other side of the garage next door. It looks like a fruit cellar entrance, but the two are connected. You'll be able to escape if you have to."

"Thank you kindly," Jennifer said. Whenever she injected herself into a conversation, it was to draw attention from Wolfe. She knew how adults could easily be distracted. It was almost uncanny, and Wolfe silently thanked her for it.

He put his goggles back in place and helped Bessie put the door down and the rug over the top. They took seats at the kitchen table and the older woman started.

"We had to do something. After the bombs, FEDCOM moved in, almost as if they were part of a plan to reshape the States. It was quick and coordinated, but we wanted to feel safe. They did that for us until they became the predators. There is no threat of invasion. We can start turning things back to the way they were. This town could take care of itself if they would only let us."

"Where did you get that flyer?" Wolfe asked, looking to find out how much the Feds knew about him.

"They had it on the wall in the post office. That was where I was going when I ran into you three." She studied her reflection in the welding goggles, imagining that Wolfe was looking at her just as keenly. "I thought it was best if no one else had a picture of you for when you're walking around."

"Much obliged," Wolfe offered. He did not care for FEDCOM in the least. Maybe the conditions *were* right for the local henchmen to meet an untimely end. "I can see like it is daylight outside. I will need you to draw me a map of the town, and where the soldiers are. I need to know how many there are. It would be best to send them somewhere else and ambush them when they are bunched up. I cannot do it alone. I will not do it alone. I have Miss Jennifer to look out for..."

Before he could continue, Jennifer jumped to her feet.

"I'm coming with you. If you don't make it, I won't either. We're family!" She didn't cry, but her lip quivered as her emotions took over. She had not shared her feelings with Wolfe. He would not have known what to do if she had. He accepted her as she was, letting her actions stand on their own. He respected her, but he did not know what bubbled deep inside. She had not talked much since her parents died.

Then again, neither had he. He did not have much to say that he had not already said. It mattered to get to Lurleen and JoJo, to see if they made it. He had to know for sure. He was not much for speculating.

"How will helping you help me get where I want to go?" Wolfe asked. That sounded harsher than he had intended, but it was the truth. If he didn't look out for himself and Jennifer, no one would. "Stirring up a hornet's nest is one more thing to run from."

"I wish I had an answer." Bessie sighed heavily. "You have weapons and everything you need. We can offer a small taste of modern conveniences. Electricity. Running water. Flush toilets. We even got toilet paper. I will feed you like royalty, and when it's time to go, you'll go with a full stomach and packs filled with food."

Jennifer looked up at Jim with big eyes. There was a clean spot on her face, but the rest was dirty. Her hair was getting matted, and her clothes needed to be washed.

"A taste of civilization sounds good after all we been through. I want Miss Jennifer cleaned up, clothes washed, and ready for church."

"We got no church, Mister. The bombs took the last of people's faith in God."

"We won't be needing a church. Just something my mother used to say. I am glad she did not see the war. She and my pop were long gone by then. Died young."

"Like my parents," Jennifer agreed before realizing what she had said.

"She's my daughter now. Her parents met with the worst misfortune, sickness. One of the body, and one of the mind. They have been gone these four or five months now. My wife and son are waiting. They will both be proud to have Jennifer join our family. And if anything happened to them, Jennifer is my only family. I will protect her with my life, and expect that you will, too. I will not abide losing her. That would not turn out well for anyone involved. And please do not take that as a threat. It is just how things will be. We do not have much, but what we have, we want to keep."

"I understand, Mister Wolfe. If you help us, you will find that maybe FEDCOM is not as all-powerful as they try to make you think they are. I see them as dominoes. Once you get the first to fall, the rest will go down one after another."

CHAPTER SIX

A dark night was a good sign. It was overcast and cool, perfect conditions for Jim Wolfe to take a walk, check on the neighbors, and scout out the Feds. He waited until sometime between two and three in the morning to give himself a couple hours. It was not a big town, but it sprawled across a fair amount of acreage. FEDCOM had the bases at both ends of the main road into and out of town.

The reason Wolfe and Jennifer had missed the soldiers on their way into town was that they came in on a side road, having walked cross-country. They could not risk the main road after what they had done to the soldiers at the crossing into the Red Zone. The soldiers here did not seem to be on high alert. Maybe they thought those two had killed each other.

Wolfe had thought his effort to cover up the crime would be less than convincing. He refused to underestimate his enemy, but maybe they deserved the low opinion he had of them, especially if they were so easily manipulated by men like the Alstons. It bothered him that his picture was down here. He thought he had gone beyond their reach. Wilders.

Scum from the Red Zone of what used to be Idaho. Wolfe thought he had made it almost to Oklahoma.

It did not matter what they called the states now. All that mattered was that he could pass through them to get back to Bradenton, Florida. If it still existed.

Wolfe walked quickly, staying in the shadows of the darkened street. His eyes drank in what light there was to make it look like the middle of the day. He knew that wasn't true, though. It was a little gray, like on a cloudy day, but that was it. The rest of the people probably never saw him.

Even though the town had electricity, they didn't bother with streetlights. Some windows were framed by the brightness of interior bulbs. Wolfe had to squint to see if anyone looked out. He circled wide of those homes to avoid casting a long shadow and being seen. He was only out to take a look. In the morning, he would use his information to start making a plan.

Bessie had not shared the exact numbers of the people in the underground. She said they only knew four names—the three in their cell, and one from another cell. That was all. In World War II, Bessie would have been a resistance fighter. She was too young to have been in any conflict, but she had the mind for it. She also had the passion.

Wolfe had left them back at the boardinghouse. They said they would await his return, but he told them all to sleep. Buddy was in bed with Jennifer. Bessie lived at the boardinghouse, but Gemini did not. He had gone home to the farm where he boarded and worked part-time. Most folks had two jobs to stay busy and keep FEDCOM supplied while also providing for themselves. Many were better off than if they had been in the Red Zone.

FEDCOM was keeping one type of scavenger out. That left them the easy pickings of a passive population. The underground had problems because there were no active soldiers left, no able-bodied veterans, no physically fit men with heads for tactics. They'd been drafted or killed.

Wolfe did not want to be anyone's last hope, but here he was, doing it anyway.

The first compound, the one to the east, had a minimum number of soldiers on hand. There was one gate, where a single soldier was sound asleep. Wolfe crept through a gap in the fence not far from the sleeper. There was no risk since he was deep in the shadows. One light bulb in the small guard shack burned brightly, blinding the guard to anything in the darkness outside. Maybe he had floodlights he could turn on, but Wolfe couldn't see them if there were.

He walked smoothly and slowly to what he determined was the barracks. Through the windows, he saw twenty bunk beds with only ten occupied, and then only the bottom bunks. Including the soldier at the gate, that meant eleven total. He continued his survey of the compound to find the locked storage area where he assumed the weapons and ammunition could be found. He noted a building he had thought was an office, but it was a duplex. When he looked through the windows, he saw couples in each of the two beds.

Wolfe sat down outside to think about what that meant. If he fired the place, he might be killing civilians. Or victims, if the women had been kidnapped. Knowing FEDCOM like he did, that was what he suspected. Prisoners, even if they didn't know it.

He checked again. They seemed to be sleeping soundly. He'd mark those buildings for personal attention. Wolfe needed to move on now. He had to get to the other side of town and back to the boardinghouse before morning.

He left the compound crouching low, moving faster than when he'd arrived. Once clear, he started jogging. It was past three, and still in the dark of night. No one was up. No lights remained on in the houses. From far off, no one would know there was a growing town here, except for the glow from the west side—the FEDCOM compound.

He ran faster, instinctively staying in the shadows. Moving across the grass to deaden his footfalls, he made great time.

The town wasn't as big as he had thought, maybe a mile from one end to the other. That meant two minutes or less travel time for a vehicle, unless it couldn't take a direct route because of barriers or spike strips in the road like the police used to use in the before time. More information to add to the planning.

As he approached, he headed into a ditch that angled toward the compound. Even in the shadows, the glaring floodlights forced him to put on his welding goggles. Wolfe moved closer to the compound, raising his head slowly over the edge so he could look for sentries or watchtowers. He saw an unoccupied tower and multiple gates, the biggest being at the main entrance up front.

There were additional gates on the sides, and although Wolfe couldn't see what was behind the buildings, he suspected there would be a gate back there, too.

Two soldiers walked back and forth across the double-vehicle-wide main gate. They were alert, and the compound was so well lit, Wolfe wouldn't dare approach. He would have to shut the lights off before he could get inside.

His advantage was also his disadvantage when the enemy had electricity and wasn't miserly about using it. Bessie, as part of the underground, might have an idea. Cutting the power because of a blown transformer would have credibility. It probably wasn't far-fetched, either. He retreated up the ditch, but a noise alerted him. Someone was coming.

Had he been followed?

He turned his head back and forth. They were coming

from the area he had just traversed. He ducked and hurried ahead, taking care to walk toe-heel to avoid making any noise. He could see the sticks and debris to avoid it, unlike those behind him, who made too much noise as they walked.

They didn't seem to be in a hurry. Two distinct sounds, and then a conversation. They were talking in hushed tones about what they would do when they finished their shift. Wolfe didn't wait to hear the rest. He ran ahead and dodged out of the ditch since he was beyond the reach of the flood-lights. He ran for cover and then slowed, moving like a shadow through the sleeping town.

When he reached the boardinghouse, he did not go in. He used the fruit cellar entrance of the next building over and found the tunnel behind a shelf that rolled easily away from the wall. He hurried through the tunnel and into the base-ment, then climbed the ladder and slowly opened the trap door. He looked through the crack under the rug and didn't see any feet, so he lifted the door the rest of the way and climbed out.

He was glad for the empty kitchen. He put everything back in place and sat down to go through in his mind every-thing he had seen.

CHAPTER SEVEN

Morning came, and with it the morning people, including Jennifer and Buddy. They immediately went outside so the dog could take care of business.

When they returned, Bessie put out a royal breakfast for Buddy. He probably did not taste the mix of meat and vegetables. Jennifer ate quickly. She was planning to soak in a hot bath. She had never had such a luxury in her life since the family cabin where she had been raised was austere. Bessie made sure she had soap and shampoo.

"You're going to scrape your skin off," Wolfe told her. She held her nose and pointed at him. "Fine. I'll shower when you're finished."

He watched her disappear into the largest of the board-inghouse's two bathrooms. Buddy ran in after her, almost knocking her over to get inside while she was trying to close the door. She shut it after him. A low thump indicated the dog finding a place to lie down. The water started to run.

Wolfe retreated to the kitchen, where Bessie was cooking bacon for him, along with making fry bread.

"I'm going to need your help," Wolfe started.

"Anything," Bessie replied before he could finish.

"The western compound was lit up like Washington DC on the Fourth of July. I couldn't get close. Do any of your people know what's in there? If so, could they maybe draw me a map and count heads? I need to know how many, where they are, and what they're doing."

"I'll have all that for you by the end of the day. When are you thinking we can rid ourselves of that filth?"

"Hold your horses, ma'am. I am still looking at things. The western compound is going to be one tough nut to crack. We can tie the eastern facility up in knots in a minute or less. Not much going on there. Do you know anything about the two women who live on that compound?"

"Women?"

"Are there any prostitutes in this town?" Wolfe asked.

Bessie rocked back on her heels as if struck. "There most assuredly are no prostitutes in Ashland, Kansas!"

Wolfe quieted and returned to his thoughts. "I meant no disrespect. I only want to know the truth. I want innocent people out of the way for when the fires start."

"You're going to burn the compound? May God have mercy on their souls."

"I don't know yet. I would prefer to be on my way, staying out of FEDCOM's sights. I never wanted to tangle with them, but those Alston brothers saw that didn't happen. Here we are now, us or them. I don't like it one bit. I just want to get home."

"I just want our home to be free," Bessie whispered.

"I look at it like driving my rig, my semi. I crossed bridges that might not have been the best, but I was willing to assume the risk if I thought they were safe. If the risk is too great, Jennifer and I will slip away under the cover of darkness. No one will ever know we were here."

Bessie bit her lip, growing paler as hope faded.

The big dog ran into the kitchen first. Wolfe caught him before he explored the counter with his tongue and held him back until Jennifer came in and took an empty seat. The dog sat next to her so she could rub his neck and scratch behind his ears.

Bessie frowned deeply. She thought Wolfe had made up his mind. "Are you leaving tonight?"

"I need to know what's in the western compound before I go anywhere. The risk. Is this a bridge we can drive across?"

Bessie perked up.

"That was the best bacon I've had in as long as I can remember," he told her as she took his plate. "And that fry bread was a work of art, ma'am."

"There's more where that came from as long, as you stick around."

"Are we leaving?" Jennifer asked innocently.

"Not if we keep feeding you," Bessie said like a grand-mother. She pushed an extra slice of bacon and a small piece of crustless fry bread toward her. Jennifer never knew her grandparents, but she believed that was how they would have been, giving her treats and making her feel like one of the princesses she had read about.

"Cookies?" she ventured.

"Miss Jennifer," Wolfe cautioned. He was not good at asking strangers for gifts. For Bessie to make something that once would have been easy would now take a great deal of effort and sacrifice. Even sugar cookies. Wolfe's mouth began to water. Lurleen's specialty was snickerdoodles. He liked chocolate chip, but in Florida, it was too hot. The chocolate would melt. Before he could stop himself, he asked, "Do you know how to make snickerdoodles?"

CHAPTER EIGHT

The smell of baking cookies drifted through the house. Wolfe almost forgot where he was. Or when. It was a different time. It was the war after the war, and that was what Wolfe had finally accepted. He did not like fighting or killing other men, but he hated what the world had become. The kind and peaceful were the targets of those who weren't.

To survive in this world, the kind and peaceful people needed a man like Jim Wolfe. He wanted to be one of them, living life with his family, putting food on the table, and pushing his son on a swing or playing ball.

Wolfe threw his legs over the edge of the top bunk and sat there to collect his thoughts. He wondered what time it was. Wolfe dragged a hand over his forever smooth face, which prevented him from gauging how long it had been since his last shower. He stepped onto the lower bunk and then to the floor. He left his pack and gear under the lower bed and made his way barefoot to the kitchen.

He stopped before he crossed the threshold. He had no boots. No weapons. No gear. He was already growing soft, and all it had taken was cookies.

And the sound of Jennifer giggling as she played with the dog to keep him from snatching a mouthful and running.

This moment represented what he was crossing the country for. He planned on walking the whole way, and it was worth it to have a normal life, with cookies.

He turned around and went back to their room, where he put on his gear, his knife, and his backpack. Wolfe returned to the kitchen and dropped the pack on the floor just inside the door, balancing the bow on top of it. Jennifer and Bessie stopped what they were doing and looked at the pack as if it were the darkest of omens.

"I have to think like I have not had to think before. I have to be ready. I cannot let myself get comfortable. Bad things happen when I take it easy. You two keep doing what you are doing. You don't want any of what I have."

Jennifer did the opposite of what he'd asked, running to him and hugging him tightly around his waist. Bessie slapped Buddy on the nose with her spatula. He yipped and backed away.

"I am with you all the way, Mister Wolfe. Where are we going?"

"*We* are going nowhere. I will go back out tonight and look the compounds over again to learn more."

Gemini appeared in the doorway, licking his lips as he looked hungrily at the cookies on the counter. It was the same look Buddy had given them. Jennifer finally let go and took a seat at the table.

"What do you have for Mister Wolfe, Gemini?"

Wolfe wanted to get the information directly from those who had seen the compound, in case he had questions. But for their security, maybe Gemini did not know who the spies were. Wolfe decided it was best to do things Bessie's way. She seemed to be a natural at the ways of the underground. He wondered how she had learned.

"Roughly one hundred twenty-five men and women. Half of those are the soldiers who perform security duties. The other half maintain the vehicles, equipment, and weapons. There are at least six officers. All of the soldiers live in the compound. The security at the gates is to protect the vehicles. Trucks and running equipment are getting rarer and rarer. That's why all the garages have to tithe; give a portion of their work to FEDCOM in spare part repair and rework."

Wolfe looked at the table as he thought about what he'd been told. Gemini dropped a piece of paper on it, a rough diagram of the FEDCOM base, buildings, parking yard, and head counts. Getting caught with something like that was a death sentence.

He had thought the so-called underground was serious, but the drawing drove it home like a nail into a cheap two by four. Wolfe studied the map.

Someone pushed a pencil into his hand. He looked at it strangely. How long had it been? He had been a big reader before the bombs, but never a writer. He did not care for his penmanship. Neither had his second-grade teacher, Mrs. Lawson. God bless her soul. She'd tried, but Wolfe's efforts looked more like voodoo symbols that a witch had etched with a crow's foot.

He roughed in the ditch near the fencing and added what he remembered about the windows. He put the pencil down and found two cookies waiting for him. Snickerdoodles.

"For you, Mister Wolfe." Bessie wiped her hands on her old apron, which was stained and faded. The kitchen was there to support a big house filled by a big family.

"Is this your home from the before time?" he asked.

"How did you know?"

He shrugged and slowly ate the first cookie, closing his eyes and thinking back to different times. A smaller kitchen in a smaller house, with a family of three. He could not remember if Lurleen's baking was better. Maybe it was. But this was a different Jim Wolfe. Scarred. Colder.

No. Not colder. More determined. Committed to protecting his family. He hadn't been there when the bombs fell. They needed money, so he had to work. He had to be all things. Fate lined up a bank shot and took him out of the picture. Lady Fate delivered her fury when he was as far away from home as he could have been.

It was time to take care of his new family and friends so he could move on. Sitting in a kitchen eating cookies wasn't getting him any closer to Bradenton. He adjusted his welder's goggles. Sometimes they still dug into his head. He wondered if he would ever be able to function without them.

"Sixty to seventy soldiers who need to know the errors of their ways," Wolfe pondered. "Can you cut power to the compound late tonight, keep it off for maybe fifteen minutes?"

"Yes, but the compound has backup generators. We used to lose power all the time, but it's probably been a year since we had any issues." Bessie knocked on the table to reinforce their good luck. But it was not luck. It was hard work by the good people of Ashland.

"Can they cut the power?" Wolfe pressed.

"Yes. I have people inside."

"What about radio or telephone? Is there any of that?"

"There is one line that connects to the west and one to the north," Bessie replied. "We used to have a person on the switchboard in their headquarters, but one day she disappeared. No one has seen her since."

"How long ago was that?"

"Sometime in the winter. Maybe six months." Bessie slid another cookie toward Wolfe. He felt like a dog getting a treat each time he did something she liked. He ate the snickerdoodle anyway.

"Pass the word to cut the power at two in the morning, and then cut it again at five. Can you do that for me, ma'am?"

"If it means ridding ourselves of FEDCOM, we will do anything you ask."

CHAPTER NINE

Jennifer refused to remain behind for the second night in a row. She had slept through the afternoon to prepare herself for it. Wolfe only had so much fight in him. Jennifer knew how to keep quiet, and she'd keep Buddy from getting out of control since she would not go anywhere without him.

Wolfe wanted it that way. If he was not there to protect her, the half-wolf would.

"I still cannot believe you ate that man's sandwich." Wolfe crouched to look the big dog in the face. "You are growing on me, but don't tell anyone."

"I won't," Jennifer assured him. She did not say anything further. Wolfe wondered what was running through her mind, but those were *her* thoughts. She would share them if she wanted to. She would probably share them if he asked, and maybe one day, he would. But that day was not today. They needed to go, make sure they were in place when the lights went out. He skipped going back to the eastern compound.

He had asked Bessie to look into the two women who had

partnered up to make sure they were there voluntarily. Still, that didn't mean they were bad. They might have been victims of circumstance. He wanted to know for sure before treating them like he would FEDCOM. Even then, he was not sure he could.

Treat women with respect. That was what his father had taught him, along with the ten commandments. Thou shalt not kill pounded in his head. Since he'd emerged from that mine shaft a year ago, the commandments had taken on a different light.

Wolfe rested his hand on Jennifer's shoulder. The new world was kill or be killed. He did not want the young girl to fall into the latter category. That meant he had to do the former. It was a sucker's choice. One or the other, and he had had enough of people he cared about being on the wrong end of violence.

"Miss Jennifer. We are going to take a look at that compound. You will do the looking for me when the lights are on, but when it goes dark, I will need to go inside their fence. You and Buddy will wait for me outside and make sure I have a way out in case they get their lights on while I'm still in there."

"Agreed, Mister Wolfe," Jennifer replied softly, as if it were a negotiation. He'd never had a daughter before and was not sure if she was acting like one was supposed to, or if she considered herself his business partner. He remained unsure, but decided that it did not matter. He hoped Lurleen liked her. And little JoJo—wherever they were.

Wolfe and Jennifer disappeared into the shadows. He held her hand and guided her. She went where he led with blind faith. Complete trust.

He tightened his grip on his AR-15. He had extra ammunition in a pouch on his belt, along with his knife; otherwise, they were traveling light.

This night, there were no houses with lights on. He kept his goggles around his neck, ready to put them on when they reached the compound. He wondered if the power had already gone out. They hurried. When they reached the outskirts of Ashland, they found the compound was already dark, but it wasn't two yet. Maybe whoever worked at the power station didn't have a reliable watch.

"Stay here!" Wolfe whispered harshly. The clock was running, and he had no idea when the alarm would ring. He reached the fence and started running along it, looking for a break or a weak spot. The guards were still at the front gate, lounging as if nothing were happening. They smoked casually and talked about nothing specific.

Cigarettes were expensive. The average soldier should not have been able to afford them, but there they were, puffing away.

Wolfe retreated. He decided to scale the fence, taking care at the top with the razor wire stretched above the top support of the chain link since he could see that the concertina had been put in place by amateurs. It was stretched too thin, and would be easy to defeat. It had to be loose, so it collapsed on itself if someone tried to step through. The barbs were designed to catch skin and clothing alike, tangling the victim in a painful embrace.

Stepping on the wire between the barbs, it stayed in place. He jumped to the other side. As soon as he hit the ground, the lights came on.

CHAPTER TEN

Wolfe flattened himself on the ground, fumbling for his goggles. He was blind until he got them into place. He hoped that becoming a dark spot in the grass would make him invisible. He faced the sentries at the main gate. They gave the thumbs up to someone inside the building.

"Looks good, Nugget," one of the two called.

They continued leaning, smoking, and talking.

Wolf started to worm his way toward the nearest shadow, moving at a snail's pace so he didn't draw anyone's eye. He hoped Jennifer and the dog stayed down, but that depended on the roving patrol. How often did they check the ditch?

I should not have brought her, he thought.

Fifteen minutes later, Wolfe found himself in the shadow of a truck. He got to his knees and crawled the last few yards until he was secure under the truck. He took the time to catch his breath and gather his wits. Keeping the truck between him and the guards, as well as him and the buildings, he waved an arm in broad strokes back into the darkness. He hoped Jennifer could see that he was okay.

He thought she might try something to save him since Wolfe had told her to make sure he could get out. He dropped to his belly and crawled under the truck. There was a great deal of room, but there was also grease. Their mechanics apparently didn't know what they were doing and used extra grease to cover up their inability to fix things in the right way, or they didn't have the right parts, greasing the wrong ones to make them work even though they did not fit.

He maneuvered between the grease mounds to get to the other side. Three more trucks, and he found himself next to the door in the main building. If the map was correct, the communications room was inside, along with the armory, kitchen, and officers' quarters. Everything important in one place. The next building was the barracks where the soldiers slept.

A plan had taken shape in his mind, but he needed to confirm a few things before he could press forward. The door had a card reader for access, a fancy security system from the before time, but the door was propped open by a rock. The security system had probably failed to open one too many times and been turned off.

He pulled the door open and slipped inside, then waited for a second as he scanned the corridor. His heart threatened to pound through his ribs. This was not something he ever wanted to get used to. He stepped lightly down the hallway, making almost no sound as he worked his way past each of the six doors, behind which were the armory, storage, and an administrative office on one side, kitchen and dining area on the other. The elevator had an out of order sign on it. A modern convenience in a small building in a small town. Wolfe never would have used it, even though he knew some people had to.

When he reached the steps, he headed up.

He climbed to the second story, finding the communications room behind the first door. It was better for him that all the doors had big windows. He figured the building might have been a school before FEDCOM took it over.

An older woman sat behind a desk, back to the door, reading a book. She wore headphones connected to an old-time switchboard panel.

Modern conveniences reinvented.

His heart continued to pound as he ducked to pass the door. Even with her back to it, she might sense the shadow passing. Wolfe did not want to take any chances. If he had to fight, any plan he had would go out the window. They needed to never suspect that he had been there. He forged ahead. The final rooms on that floor had been converted into the officers' quarters, six of them behind four doors. Handwritten nameplates had been taped to the doors to signify who was inside. Two to each room except the last one, which was labeled as guest quarters. Someone was shuffling around inside that room.

Wolfe took the rifle off his shoulder and held it ready.

The other three rooms were as silent as a graveyard. He peeked through the gap in the old newspapers that had been secured over the window. His pounding heart slowed with the chill that crept over him. A man was sitting on the couch. He yawned and scratched the stubble on his face before lying down and rolling his back toward the door.

An Alston brother not fifteen feet from him.

Two others were in the bunk bed against the far wall. Wolfe squinted, trying to figure out if it was the other Alston who slept in the bed. He could not be sure. And the third figure. Was that the major? He had forgotten the man's name. All three of them were scum, and he hated them equally.

Wolfe's mouth twisted into the snarl of his namesake. He could break through that door with no effort at all. He could kill them right there, the Alstons and their FEDCOM partner in crime. But that would not be the end of it. There were other soldiers. How could he finish them all?

The snarl turned into an ugly smile. Wolfe didn't like his dark thoughts, but he had them all the same. He saw an ending where he was standing over their dead bodies and telling them, "I should have killed you all back then." That was when he had still believed his fellow men had honor. The Alstons had taught him differently. And the major.

Had they followed Wolfe all the way down here? How was that possible?

Wolfe didn't believe in coincidences. He checked the corridor and backed away from the door, then turned toward the end of the hallway. The small light in the communication room went out with the power. It was two in the morning.

CHAPTER ELEVEN

Wolfe started to run, then stopped and crouched below the window of the communications door. He stood up once he was past the door and quickly covered the remaining distance to the stairs. When the door opened, the older woman looked back and forth as if she thought she saw something. She went back inside to check her equipment.

Wolfe had frozen on the stairs when he heard the door open. When it shut again without footfalls coming toward him, he took the steps three at a time, hitting the bottom landing and flexing his knees when he touched down to absorb the shock and keep the sound to a gentle tap. He was off again instantly, running fast for the far door. He slid to a stop, one boot leaving a black skid mark. A real military would have someone buff that out first thing in the morning. This ragtag mob? He doubted they would even notice.

He went sideways out the door to keep it from opening too wide, but it was dark outside, the pitch-black kind of dark that happens when the moon is behind heavy clouds. Wolfe said a quick thank you and ducked to look under the trucks for the feet of sentries. Once he was sure they were clear, he jogged on his toes, making no sound as he ran for the fence. Up and over he went. Wolfe hit the ground on the other side and froze, expecting the lights to come back on, but they did not.

Wolfe ran for the ditch and hopped over the edge to land next to Jennifer. The dog yipped, and Jennifer jumped.

"Shhh," Wolfe whispered. "It's only me. Let's go."

He took the young girl by the hand and they loped down the ditch, heading away from the compound. A heavy engine started up, a truck. The headlights turned on, pointing toward the main gate. A second motor ground to life, and shortly thereafter, the floodlights crept back into existence. It had taken no more than five minutes for the Feds to get the lights on.

Why had they been off earlier?

Too many questions. Too many coincidences. Wolfe and Jennifer went straight back to the boardinghouse, but they did not go in. They waited outside, where they could see without being seen. Jennifer curled up on the ground under a bush, with Buddy squeezed in beside her. Wolfe watched with his naked eyes, enjoying the darkness while watching for an ambush from the boardinghouse.

But nothing happened. The home remained dark until the first tendrils of morning crawled over the horizon to greet him and make him put his goggles on. He left Jennifer behind as he made a circuit, listening at the door of the fruit cellar in case a group waited there. No one waited. In the boardinghouse, Bessie was busying herself in the kitchen.

When Wolfe returned to the sleeping girl, Buddy's head was up, and he was watching.

"Good boy. You know your job. What do you say we sneak you a slice of bacon and then get some shut-eye?" Wolfe slung his rifle over his back and carefully picked Jennifer up, and she snuggled into to his chest without waking up. He hurried through the shadows, up the front porch, and inside while it was still too dark for normal people to see. The dog followed him through, letting the door slam louder than he wanted.

He stopped in his tracks and glared at the dog. Buddy sniffed once, and with tongue lolling, headed for the kitchen.

"Hide the bacon. The dog's coming," Wolfe called toward the open kitchen door.

"Get out of here, you thieving hound!" Bessie shouted before he heard the sound of a spatula smacking a dog's rump. Buddy ran past, carrying a slab of bacon in his mouth. With his arms full of the young girl, the best he could do was try to trip the dog, but that failed. Buddy ran under the table and started chewing. That ended any hope for breakfast bacon.

"I apologize, Miss Bessie," Wolfe said when the woman appeared. He did not say anything else. He was not going to promise to replace the meat. He did not know if he could. "Thank you for turning off the power. They have a backup generator. The lights came back on after about five minutes."

She looked at him closely. "Was that enough time to get what you needed?"

"The lights were off when we got there. I thought your person at the power station had gone early, but then the power went out exactly at two."

"They test things on occasion. Maybe that's what it was."

"The sentries did not seem to mind, but I saw someone I know in the compound. He is from Idaho, the Red Zone. Would you have any idea why he is here?"

"Is he a friend?" Bessie asked. The glare Wolfe gave her told her what he thought of the question, although the steel in his eyes remained hidden behind the dark lenses of the welding goggles. "I did not know there were any visitors here, Mister Wolfe. They don't tell us things like that, and none of my people heard anything. At least, they weren't able to pass the information along."

"We would like to get some sleep, and then I need to think. Do you have any maps of Ashland and the surrounding area?"

"One." Bessie went to the check-in counter and opened a drawer. She carefully handed the old map over. "They burned almost everything."

Wolfe frowned. No wonder there were so few books. It was yet another way for FEDCOM to control people.

"Sleep first. Then we will talk. Privately."

CHAPTER TWELVE

Jennifer got up around midday to take Buddy outside. Wolfe noted their departure and rolled over to go back to sleep. A commotion outside a few minutes later made him shoot upright. He leaped from the top bunk, landing softly on the floor. He put his goggles in place, pulled the heavy curtains aside, and looked at the yard. He caught sight of the big dog at the edge of the house. He couldn't see Jennifer, but she would not be far from Buddy.

The dog's hackles were up, and he was growling at something Wolfe couldn't see. He pulled on his boots and grabbed his rifle, running into the hall and down the stairs. He stopped when he hit the landing and pressed himself against the wall. Bessie was outside, and she was yelling. Wolfe craned his neck to see where they were.

He edged closer to a corner so he could look out. The front door burst open, and Jennifer and the dog ran in. Bessie backed in, yelling at someone he could not see. She slammed the door and locked it.

Wolfe tried to see past her, but she yanked the curtains over the front door window.

"Come on. Get your stuff. Time for us to go," Wolfe told Jennifer, remaining on the stairs as she climbed past him.

"It's not that," Bessie said. Someone started pounding on the front door.

"It sounds like exactly that."

Jennifer returned while the pounding continued, along with angry shouts. She thrust his bag into his hands, including his bow.

"Basement," he whispered, and they ran, hunched over, to the kitchen. He opened the hidden door, and she went down. With his pack over one shoulder, he picked up the dog with one arm, even as big as the hairy beast was. Wolfe's strength was immense. It was like carrying a small bag for him. He picked his way down the ladder and set the dog down, then climbed back up and pulled the rug to the edge of the door, flipping it as he pulled the door closed.

But they had seen Jennifer and the dog. Their disappearance would make whoever was trying to get in suspicious if they made it past Bessie. The old girl was putting up a stalwart verbal fight.

Wolfe pointed toward the tunnel and Jennifer took the dog. He followed close behind. They moved the secret wall and closed it behind them. Wolfe held his finger to his lips. He put his pack and bow down but kept the AR-15 with him. He cracked the fruit cellar door and peeked out. Since it faced the boardinghouse, he could see everything that was going on. A FEDCOM Jeep was parked at the curb.

"What happened?" Wolfe whispered over his shoulder.

"They wanted to take Buddy away from me," Jennifer replied, huffing as if getting ready to cry.

"What else?"

"Miss Bessie ran out and stopped them. Started calling them names. I got inside, and she closed the door in their ugly faces."

Wolfe nodded as he watched. Two men. They did not seem to be very angry. Wolfe could hear Bessie, but not the exact words. She was fired up.

"How about some home-baked bread?" one of them called while leaning on the vehicle.

Her shout back made Wolfe blush. He looked to see if Jennifer had heard, but she was sniffling and had both hands deep in Buddy's long hair.

The door to the boardinghouse opened, and a small loaf of bread flew out and hit the closest soldier in the chest. He fumbled it once, twice, and seized it before it hit the ground. He waved at the house, gave half to his partner in crime, and they both climbed back into their vehicle. They drove off, elbows out the window, casually.

"It's clear. We can go back now."

Bessie was waiting with the door open when they reached the boardinghouse basement. Wolfe sent Jennifer first before he looped an arm around the dog and climbed up to the kitchen.

"Their idea of fun?" Wolfe asked evenly.

"You can't give them an inch. They would have ransacked this house had I let them in."

"We can't have that, now can we, Miss Bessie?" Wolfe checked the time. "Where is Gemini?"

"He is off today."

Wolfe shook his head and went to the refrigerator. There was a sealed bottle inside that looked like a beer.

"Jumping at shadows, Mister Wolfe?" Bessie asked. He didn't answer. "Go ahead, take the beer. I know where I can get more. It might not be what you're used to."

"What I'm used to is nothing. It's better than that. Where did you get your coffee?"

"Chicory, dandelion root, and some other things. It's not real coffee. I'd kill for a cup of the good stuff." Bessie chuckled. Her skin had started to regain its color. She was too old to fight with the younger generation.

"That was a good throw. You hit him right in the chest."

"I was aiming for the bullseye between his legs."

Wolfe decided it was better to let it go. He took the beer, thanking Bessie as he popped it open using only his fingers, instinctively turning sideways to the old woman.

CHAPTER THIRTEEN

"Do you think we should?" Bessie asked. Wolfe would not have requested the meeting with members of the underground if there had been another way.

"I need five things to happen at once, and I can only do two of them," he said for the third time. "It is important that I talk with them together since they need to work together. It is like loading a truck. More hands can make it easier or harder, depending on how they coordinate the work."

"Please don't get me wrong, Mister Wolfe. I don't mind that you see them. I'm worried about them seeing each other. It will change how they treat each other when they go about their daily business. It puts the underground at risk."

"After tomorrow, I do not think it will matter. Everything will change, for better or worse." Wolfe took his piece of paper and sketched the timeline of the coming night's actions. "Has anyone in the underground killed another human being?"

"We have a couple old fellas who are veterans, but I don't know if they ever went anywhere. We'll have to ask them."

"Bring them. Anything is better than nothing. We'll need

a young woman who can run, and two bikes. We'll need men who can throw. We'll need someone who can climb. We'll need people who aren't afraid to shoot a gun," Wolfe said softly. Gemini leaned in the doorway so he could be part of the conversation, as well as watch the front door. If someone came in, he was there to keep them occupied until Wolfe could disappear. He'd been seen when he'd first entered Ashland, but not since. He wanted to keep it that way.

Keep the bad guys guessing. Although he did not want the Alstons to move on. It was time for a reckoning. He shook the anger from his head and started roughing out his plan.

"The challenge is sending the soldiers from the western compound on a wild goose chase that ends in a trap. It starts with the eastern compound after we've sent people far to the west."

"I don't understand," Bessie muttered. "We go west and east to focus on the western compound?"

Wolfe helped himself to the pad of paper on the table. He drew two columns and labeled them East Compound and West Compound. He added times down the left-hand side, then filled in actions. It looked like a vertical trucker's logbook, with annotations stating what was supposed to happen and how long each segment would take. Multiple actions overlapped.

"I don't see how you're going to do all of that." Bessie shook her head vigorously.

The old woman had been on top of things, but Wolfe was starting to wonder. "That is what the members of the underground are going to help me with. After I meet everyone, I will ask for volunteers for each of the jobs that need to be done. They take skills, but as long as they are giving their best, that is all anyone can ask." Wolfe's voice trailed off. He had the strength and speed to get himself out of a bad situation. The volunteers with the underground didn't. They were the elderly, the women, and even children.

The healthy men had been drafted and sent away. Wolfe suspected that meant the ones who did not go over to the FEDCOM way were dealt with in the harshest way, their bodies left in ditches for the vultures.

"When are they coming?"

"Ten," Bessie replied. "Another few hours before they get here."

"Someone will see them since people do not usually move around at night. I didn't see anyone roaming the streets."

"There is no other way. This is the biggest place we have complete control over."

Wolfe started to fret. He stood and paced, looking out the windows as he passed. He was not sure what he expected to see. The Feds were keeping to themselves, and that caused him some concern. He expected they were up to no good. By not being outside, he could not see what they were doing, and not knowing was digging at him. So much depended on avoiding the FEDCOM soldiers.

"Relax, Mister Wolfe. The good people of Ashland know how to handle the soldiers. Usually, they just give in to whatever the soldiers want, no matter how foul. One more time is not going to kill anyone."

"It might just kill the soldiers, though," Gemini added grimly.

CHAPTER FOURTEEN

W olfe had moved to the shadows. Even with his welding glasses on, he found more comfort in the darkness.

The meeting had just ended, and the first people were getting ready to head out, a brother and sister on bikes. They were younger than he wanted, but they had volunteered, and had the energy to ride ten to twenty miles.

The girl was dressed like a boy in ill-fitting men's clothes and had short-cropped hair to avoid unwanted attention from the soldiers. She had the voice Wolfe wanted, along with the wiry frame to climb the pole. Wolfe handed the young man a small toolkit and a wired phone that Bessie had acquired earlier.

"One more time," Wolfe coaxed.

"Emergency! Wilders are attacking the Red Zone crossing. Bring everyone to stop them. Please hurry!" She smiled innocently after she had finished.

"Can you lower your voice and sound older?"

She ran through it again.

"Exactly like that, and then cut the main wire. Thank you,

miss. Exactly at five in the morning." Wolfe looked at the watches they both wore. They held them up to show they had the correct time. "And then get yourselves out of there. Stay off the main roads. When the convoy passes, get yourselves home. We will take care of the rest."

The two nodded and left. Wolfe watched them through a crack in the curtains. They jumped on their bikes and started riding. Too fast, he thought. It was dark out. But they were excited. They would slow down soon enough.

He hoped they would.

Wolfe wanted Jennifer to stay safely with Bessie, but the old woman had said she was coming, too. She wanted to see it through. Like a general sending her army to fight an enemy, Bessie insisted on being there. Wolfe could not talk her out of it. "You stay together," he told her and Jennifer. Wolfe did not have to worry about the big dog.

Bessie cornered Wolfe while he was by himself, lost in his thoughts.

"It's too late for anything except giving it the best we got."

"Blood will be spilled before the sun rises. I do not like any of it," Wolfe confided. "But it must be done. Let it be more of theirs than ours."

"I cannot thank you enough for helping us, Mister Wolfe. We hope to convince you to help us get settled once FEDCOM is out of the picture. If you can't stay, we will load you up and have you on your way as soon as we can."

Wolfe nodded. His mind drifted to Lurleen and JoJo.

"If I didn't know better. I'd say you were thinking about someplace nicer than here. Care to share your thoughts?" Bessie asked.

"Florida. My wife and son. I have to believe they are waiting for me."

"If they aren't, you are always welcome here," Bessie said softly while squeezing Wolfe's arm.

That wasn't what he wanted to hear, but it would have to do.

"What happens when other FEDCOM units come to see what happened to their people?" Wolfe wondered.

That train had already left the station. They might show up tomorrow, for all he knew. But his promise to himself had been to live more for today and less for the next since too much rolled across his path that he had no control over. He was hanging on for the ride, and with Jennifer to look out for, he could not get distracted.

Or starry-eyed. Protecting her meant building a wall around her, one that held back the men like the soldiers from FEDCOM. He would not let them get near her.

But they had. And Miss Bessie had fought them off.

He needed more friends like her. Jennifer needed her freedom, and he was only one man. He could not watch her all the time. She had to learn to fend for herself, just in case something happened to him.

Wolfe closed his eyes and tried to calm his wandering mind. There was too much to think about. Too many questions, and not enough answers.

"I'll leave you to it," Bessie told him, finally letting go of his arm.

He watched her go from person to person, delivering words of encouragement to each of the groups as they stood around and talked. Three more teams would head out shortly to get in place for the delivery of their early morning surprise.

Two old men slowly approached Wolfe.

"Excuse us, Mister. We both served in the Army and are ready to go. We might have some skills you need."

"Can you make a Molotov cocktail?" he asked.

One of the men smiled. "A little laundry soap, gasoline, and a rag for a wick. I can do that. Just need some gasoline."

Bessie had heard from the other side of the basement. "How about some high-test grain alcohol?"

"You told me…" His words ended as Bessie smiled at him. "Why, you old hag!"

"If you had known, you would have been bugging me something fierce for a bottle or three to throw down that bottomless gullet of yours."

"I might have done just that, but now that I know, you won't be able to hide it from me."

Bessie gestured for him to follow her. The other man stayed.

"He didn't learn that when we served," the man said. "He loved burning things and blowing stuff up. Well, what soldier doesn't?"

Wolfe nodded. He had not served, and did not know what soldiers liked or not. The only soldiers he had had any contact with were the ones from FEDCOM, and they were the refuse of humanity in his mind. He knew there had to be a different side. The old codgers showed him what could have been. Enjoying life without getting into other people's business.

"During your talk, you asked about other things an old soldier might do. I can shoot a mortar and a heavy machine-gun. There ain't much call for that stuff around here, but I saw they have 'em. I'm not sure they know how to use 'em. Seem kinda young for that training."

Wolfe examined the old man. "Everyone looks young the older we get," Wolfe noted.

The old man laughed himself into a wheezing cough. His face turned red, then he stopped and dragged a sleeve across his mouth. "Ain't that the truth. Don't make me laugh, mister. It never turns out well, but damn, that was funny."

CHAPTER FIFTEEN

Wolfe abandoned all pretense of traveling in the shadows. The vast mob behind him was making too much noise. They walked in the open where they could see. Some of them were talking.

He ducked into a driveway that went between two darkened houses. The thirty people behind him followed. Wolfe turned at the end and held up his hands.

"This is not going to work. You are making too much noise." As if to emphasize his point, Buddy dove into the bushes and wrestled with something before emerging victorious, a ground squirrel in his mouth.

"I need you." Wolfe pointed to the two old veterans. "I need you four." More pointing. "And you two. Bessie, you take Jennifer and everyone else to a place near the road leading into the eastern compound. Once we have everything in hand, we will need everyone to come in and help us carry any arms and ammunition they have. We cannot leave anything there."

"Kill 'em all. Let God sort 'em out," the old soldier said.

Wolfe could not sympathize with him. He did not want to kill anyone. He was only doing what he had to do.

And that had changed since he walked out of that shaft, which seemed like a lifetime ago. With his goggles around his neck, he could see in the dark as if it were hazy twilight. He could bend steel, and his hair had turned white. He had dyed it brown, but it was growing again, and the white roots were starting to show.

He would have to find more dye unless he finished the Alstons and the major. Removed them and their ability to haunt him.

There was so much he would change if he could, from driving the truck to after the fall. Letting men like the Alstons have their way made everyone worse. They needed to be corralled and broken. They needed to be a footnote in history, not making history.

Their time had come.

Wolfe would see to that this very night. His lip twitched into a feral snarl that no one could see. It was too dark for that.

"Time to go," he told his small group. "Miss Bessie, stay back a ways. Let us have the road. You'll know when it is okay to cut the wire and join us."

She produced a hacksaw blade and pair of wire cutters. "We'll take care of it. How will I know when it's time to go?"

"I reckon the noise and shouting will tell you." Wolfe hoisted his bow. He had eight arrows in his quiver. He was running low again. He did not want to waste them but had no choice.

Too many times recently, he had had no choice. It was like hanging onto the raft as it raced down the rapids. He was not even sure he was riding on the inside.

Wolfe led the group to the edge of the small fenced compound. This time, the sentry at the front gate was wide awake. He peered into the darkness while leaning against the barricade that blocked the main gate. Wolfe motioned for everyone behind him to get down.

Wolfe nocked an arrow, took aim, and held it steady as he crept forward. He had to make a clean shot since he could not risk the sentry crying out. One step after another, carefully, toe first, then heel. A crack of something underfoot. The sentry's head snapped toward Wolfe. The man started to bring up his gun, and Wolfe loosed the arrow.

It raced home, burying itself to the feathers in the sentry's throat. Wolfe ran forward, accelerating at the unnatural speed that had come with his great strength. He caught the man before he tumbled to the ground. Wolfe pulled the arrow out, looking around as he cleaned it and prepared it for another shot. He studied the area.

Like last time, there was only one sentry and no lights.

Wolfe waved his arm in exaggerated circles to catch the attention of those behind him. They rose slowly and cautiously approached. A couple of the women could not take their eyes off the body. The blood dripping from the gory neck-wound reflected the dim light of the crescent moon.

"Stay here, and watch for anyone coming. Raise the alarm if you see anyone," Wolfe whispered to one of the women. He pushed the rest past the barrier into the compound. He pointed at the building that had held the two couples. "Secure that one, and pull the women out and find if they are there by choice. Secure the men." He led the others to the small barracks.

It was the same as before.

Wolfe nodded at the two Molotov cocktails the old soldier carried. The man winked back.

The woman at the front gate started screaming and pointing. Someone inside the barracks started to yell. The old man flicked a lighter, blinding Wolfe. He covered his face and backed away.

The next thing he knew, the window had broken under the force of the thrown bottle. The second one followed the first through.

Wolfe pulled his goggles into place and blinked to clear the bright flashes from his eyes and the piercing pain from his head. Someone popped through a door next to him. His instincts honed from a year on the road through the Red Zone, where everything and everyone seemed to want him dead, he caught the individual by the throat, shook him until his neck bones snapped, and threw him back through the doorway, blocking two others from escaping. He shut the door, and held it against their efforts. The screaming started. The pounding subsided. And then only the crackle of the fire remained.

"Put that fire out," Wolfe growled. He hurried to the other building, where the second team had their four sleepy captives in hand. The women were half-naked and the men in their underwear. All were angry at the intrusion.

The old veteran saluted before speaking. "We have determined that all four are FEDCOM sympathizers!" he declared in a firm voice.

Wolfe frowned at the term.

"What are we supposed to do with you?" Wolfe asked.

The one who has snarling less raised his head and threw his shoulders back. "I demand that you release us."

"I would love to do that, but you see, FEDCOM is a bunch of raping, thieving murderers. Since you're wearing their uniform, seems like you threw your lot in with the wrong side. Too many decent people around here to leave your kind to run roughshod."

One of the captive women belted out an expressive list of

curse words attacking Wolfe and his lineage. Wolfe finally tired of her creativity.

"And what's up with those stupid goggles, freak?" she ended.

"I'm not one for hitting women, but if I were, you would be a prime candidate."

"These four are going to be a problem. Should we execute them?" the old soldier asked.

The expression of disdain disappeared and the color drained from the men's faces. Miss Bessie arrived with the other underground volunteers in tow. The foul-mouthed woman started screeching and Bessie back-handed her across the face hard enough to knock her down.

"Maybe I was wrong, Mister Wolfe. This town does have prostitutes."

The second woman broke free and lunged for the old woman, but Buddy had other ideas. He launched himself at her, catching the hooker mid-stride and dragging her down by the throat. Jennifer didn't blink as the dog finished the woman. No one raised a hand to help her, not even the two male captives. The second woman crawled backward to put distance between her and the half-wolf Angel of Death.

Another volunteer stopped her and dragged her to her feet. "You better mind your manners," Bessie warned.

"With me," Wolfe directed, leaving the captives to the old woman as he took a group to the building he thought was the armory. He gripped the lock and hasp, braced himself, and pulled. It resisted, but it couldn't withstand everything Wolfe gave it. The metal snapped, and the door opened.

Wolfe removed his goggles to look inside. He was disappointed to see only a dozen M16 rifles, no more than a thousand rounds of 5.56mm ball ammo, and twenty empty magazines. There were two M1911A1 pistols with two magazines and a single box with fifty ACP cartridges.

"Load these up and give them to anyone willing to shoot. Give them a quick class on how to operate these rifles," Wolfe told his two veterans. With his goggles back over his eyes, he flipped the switch and the lights came on.

Half a dozen volunteers squeezed into the room and started filling magazines.

CHAPTER SIXTEEN

Wolfe wouldn't let them leave the bodies on the ground. They hauled them into the half-burned barracks, tossed them inside, and closed the door. It was a cinder-block building with a steel door, now warped from the heat. Those inside had never had a chance.

Jennifer wiped Buddy's muzzle with a rag lying on the ground. Bessie stayed close, directing traffic and telling everyone to keep the noise down.

"They have a truck," one of the old veterans said.

"You can grab it after this is all over. For now, we still need surprise on our side."

"And that's why you wanted us to put out the fire," another man commented.

"And cut the telephone wire," Bessie added.

Wolfe looked into the darkness. With his welding glasses on, it looked dark to him, too. "I'll be right back." Jennifer and Buddy stayed at his side. She hung onto the bow hanging over his shoulder. At the edge of the compound, he pulled off his goggles. In the far distance, he could see the glow from the floodlights of the western compound.

The trio returned to the others. "Time?" he asked.

"Four-thirty," Bessie answered.

"Let's move," he called loudly. "Quiet, now. We are going to sneak up on them and watch the soldiers leave, and then we need to take over that compound. Anyone left should not be the fighting type."

Bessie leaned close. "It made sense before, but now that we're out here, how sure are you that all their fighting types will leave and we can waltz right in there?"

"I was never much of a dancer, ma'am," Wolfe replied. He did not want to tell her the truth: that his plan revolved around luck, hope, and surprise. "It has to work. It was the only plan I could come up with."

"Better than anything we had," she conceded. "What do we do with those three?"

"I'll take care of it," one of the women from the underground said.

"You know these…individuals?"

"That one." She pointed to the woman who had spoken earlier. The look on her face said it had not been a pleasant encounter.

"Give her the pistol," Wolfe said in a cold and hard voice. The .45 caliber fired a big slug at a slower speed. It was loud up close, but the supersonic crack was the sound that carried.

"We better get going. I will be out front. Please keep them quiet, especially as we get close." Wolfe could not risk the group being discovered. After what they had done at the eastern compound, they would all be put to death. FEDCOM took no prisoners. He had seen that personally.

He moved far enough away from the group to be able to take off his goggles, then waved for them to follow him through the front gate and to the side roads that led through the town. A block away, he heard a loud pop, followed by two more. Then silence.

Wolfe stopped and said a short prayer for the woman who could execute people like that. He had known she was going to do it, and had given her the tool to carry it out. The deaths were every bit as much on his head as theirs. All four of them. He could have stopped Buddy but didn't. He wondered how *he* would be treated when he arrived at the Pearly Gates. He suspected he would never get that close. He rubbed his eyes.

The bombs had changed everything. A war where he never knew what happened to start it, but was painfully aware of what finished it. He figured both sides had lost, as well as all the people the government was supposed to be protecting.

And that had given birth to FEDCOM. He could no longer stand by and let them have their way. That woman was carrying out justice for a crime against her. An eye for an eye. Wasn't that what the Good Book said?

After the night sounds returned without any sign that FEDCOM soldiers had heard the gunfire, he started walking again.

CHAPTER SEVENTEEN

Wolfe held up his fist like he had seen in the movies back when there were movies. The people behind him should have stopped, but they did not. He turned around and walked toward them, waving his arms. When they finally saw him, they froze in their tracks. He held out his hands in a gesture that said, "Stay."

He headed back to the last house on the street, staying behind a heavily overgrown hedge. He worked his way past the branches and leaves until he could see the compound. With his goggles on, he looked from one side to the other, and from bottom to top. There was nothing different from the last time he was there. He backed carefully out of the bushes and hurried to Bessie.

"Can you shut the power off after the convoy pulls out?"

"I didn't coordinate that!" the woman almost shouted in exasperation.

Wolfe tried to calm her. "I know. It's okay. I think that could give us the edge we need. If you can't, we'll deal with it."

He kicked himself for not thinking that part of the plan

through. This was the point where the soldiers might shoot back.

"We cannot see in the dark like you, Mister Wolfe," Bessie said softly.

That was why he had not included it in the plan. The underground needed to be able to see. Speed was their friend.

"Wait here. I'll take another look."

He returned to his spot and counted the guards on duty. Only the two at the front gate. No roving patrol that he could see, but he suspected they were out there. They could be sleeping. The FEDCOM soldiers had little discipline. When one of their officers had a boot up their backside, they could get them going in one direction. Otherwise, they were barely above animals.

It made Wolfe wonder about the gate guards. Why were the western compound guards on their toes? The other compound had had one guard sleeping and one awake. Maybe the officers were there with a big stick? The soldiers were doing what they were told under threat of punishment.

Maybe that was why the soldiers wanted to control the civilians, stealing every aspect of their lives because it was their only chance to be in charge. It made them feel important.

The day of reckoning had arrived. For FEDCOM and the Alstons.

"Why are you here?" he whispered. He had not had anyone watch the compound since he first saw an Alston brother. He had no way to know if they were still there. He expected they would go with the convoy if they were. He hoped he would see them drive out.

He was counting on it.

Time marched on, heading toward five in the morning. False dawn suggested it was close. Wolfe could have asked someone since he did not wear a watch, but he did not live his life that way. He lived by daylight and darkness. Maybe he would try to find a watch for Jennifer. She would need to know the time to live like a normal person.

Unlike him.

Floodlights mercilessly lit the area. Even with the goggles, if Wolfe looked directly at the beams, it pained him.

Someone shouted from inside the big building, the one Wolfe had gone into on his visit. The one with the officers' quarters.

He squinted to focus on the windows and watch for movement. An alarm started to scream. Like an air raid siren, it wailed louder and louder. People raced from the barracks, but there was no direction. They stood around in the open area of the compound. When a uniformed officer ran from the big building, he started shouting orders. The men and the few rough-looking women of FEDCOM jumped into the trucks, starting them one by one until they were all running.

The plan had been implemented. He hoped those kids had cut the wire and were running for their lives. They did not need the soldiers to find them anywhere near the road.

Wolfe needed the convoy to go all the way to the Red Zone. He had to have that time, especially with the group hiding in a yard behind him.

He silently encouraged the soldiers to join the parade away from the compound, but the gate guards looked like there were going to stay put. They had their weapons across their chests while they waited to raise the gate.

There! From the big building. The Alston brothers and the major.

All three together.

They looked around, far warier than their local counterparts. Wolfe instinctively backed farther into the hedge. Soldiers streamed from the barracks, taking a detour into the big building where the armory was and emerging with M16s. They climbed into the backs of the trucks and waited.

The officer who had been doing the shouting ran from truck to truck before climbing into the cab of one of the vehicles at the front. The convoy rolled out, the gate guards letting them through. The Alstons stood away from the last truck in line. Wolfe focused on them. Then someone waved from within the canvas-shrouded back. The truck lurched to a stop, and the three men climbed in. The engine revved, then the truck jerked into gear and followed the others onto the road.

The two gate guards watched the trucks go. A man and a woman in white aprons stood in the doorway to the big building, wiping their hands as they watched their breakfast crowd disappear into the distance. They returned inside. That left two. The floodlights glared into the first tinges of dawn. Wolfe judged the distance as too far for his bow.

He didn't want to use his rifle but was left with no choice. He checked it to make sure it was ready to fire, then loped away from the hedge, angling toward the closest section of fence. The guards were turned away and had not seen him. He jogged easily toward the gate, staying close to the fence, out of their sight. He realized he'd be able to reach them without having to fire his weapon, so he sprinted, running as fast as he could to close the distance.

When they realized he was behind them, they nearly fell backward in surprise. He used the AR-15 as a club, braining the first one before grappling with the second. He broke the man's wrist bones with a squeeze and a twist. As the soldier started to scream, Wolfe let go and punched him in the face hard enough to crack his skull. The sounds of his pain died on his lips. He fell in a heap next to his dead companion. Wolfe waved to the crowd.

This time they could see him. The group of thirty or so

ambled toward him. He started issuing orders, pointing to pairs of people with each command. Jennifer came up next to him and he put a protective arm over her shoulder.

"Take their weapons and stay here. You, check the barracks. You two, around back. My veterans, come with me. We have the dining facility to secure and the armory to open."

CHAPTER EIGHTEEN

The rock was still on the ground, propping the door open. Wolfe flung the door wide and walked through. The armory was locked, but the doors to the kitchen and dining room were open. He strolled into the kitchen area, where the two cooks were preparing the morning meal for the soldiers.

"Good morning. I am going to need you to leave the compound for a bit," Wolfe said, tipping his head in a friendly greeting. Jennifer grabbed Buddy before he could help himself to the food lining the counter.

"Who are you?" the man asked, stopping mid-whip while holding a huge bowl of eggs.

Wolfe looked down at himself. A rifle in his hand. A bow and quiver over his shoulder. His welding goggles up, and his long brown hair covering his ears and falling to his shoulders.

"I'm Jim Wolfe, and I need you to leave." It was plain and straightforward. There was no sense in mincing words.

"Or what?" the man shot back, but his words were weak

and his shoulders sagged. The woman put down what she was working on.

"Sounds like we're off early today, Bill." She took the pan from his hands and set it on the counter. "Time to go."

"Take her advice, and you'll save yourself a lot of grief. You don't want to be here when the soldiers return."

"What's going to happen?" the cook named Bill asked.

"A reckoning," Wolfe replied. One of the old veterans encouraged the cooks to hurry up by nudging them with the barrel of his rifle. Once they were gone, Wolfe went to the armory.

The heavy padlock resisted even his strength as he tried to pull it open with his bare hands. One of the old men said, "I saw something on the way in. Hang on." He tottered down the hallway and went outside, returning after a few seconds carrying a crowbar. "A mechanic's friend."

Wolfe took it and made short work of the lock, then pulled the heavy steel door open. He flicked the switch inside the door to reveal all that they would have when the soldiers returned.

It wasn't what Wolfe had hoped. Three rifles remained, and several crates of 5.56mm ammunition. He had been hoping for something heavier.

The old vet sensed his angst.

"They wouldn't put the good stuff in here. There's probably a different storage area that they can get to from the outside. Soldiers wouldn't mess up the nicely buffed corridor floor by dragging an Mk19 grenade launcher down here."

"A grenade launcher?" Wolfe asked.

"Those trucks all had the pintle mounts. They probably would have taken them if they had their wits about them. The fifty cals, too."

"We need to find them and quickly," Wolfe told the man. The old soldier saluted and hurried away. Wolfe laid the crowbar over his shoulder and walked upstairs. He stopped at the communications room, where a young woman now sat. When she saw Wolfe, fear seized her, and she started to silent scream while holding her face.

Wolfe opened the door. "I need you to leave the compound, ma'am. Go on. You do not want to be here for what is coming."

Unlike the cooks, that was good enough for her. She grabbed her handbag using a well-practiced motion and flew past Wolfe on her way out.

Wolfe checked the remaining rooms to make sure they were empty before returning downstairs. He found the old soldier waiting. "We'll need you to get the door open."

The old man led the way around the building. While they were walking, Wolfe took stock of the situation. There were too few from the underground. He saw six people, and only half of them were carrying weapons. One rifle did not have a magazine inserted.

He turned back to the matter at hand. The outside door had a lock similar to the one inside. With the pry bar and a vicious twist, he broke it open. Everything he had been hoping for was inside. The old veteran cheered.

Wolfe stopped the old man before he could grab anything. "You remember the plan. Only weapons we can put into place and fire effectively. I do not know how any of this stuff works." He gestured toward the array of firepower within the vault.

"But we do, Mister Wolfe." The two veterans nodded vigorously. "We know what to do. Send us the people, and we will set up an ambush that will free us from FEDCOM once and for all."

Wolfe nodded and let the old men begin the process of removing the heavy weapons they could use. Wolfe looked for Bessie. She would find and send the volunteers. Wolfe wanted to know what was happening on the road. He wanted to know how much time he had, but would not be getting that information.

They had to be ready when the convoy returned. It felt like they had already taken too long and were behind schedule.

"Miss Jennifer," Wolfe started, "please find Bessie and ask her to bring the volunteers to us here. This is what we were looking for. We have a lot of work in front of us and no time to do it."

"I'll take care of it, Mister Wolfe," the young girl told him confidently.

She ran off, with Buddy on her heels. Wolfe knew she would do as she'd said. He found that he trusted her completely. She was family.

He heard her yelling, and soon people came running out of the barracks, then more. Wolfe could only laugh despite the tension twisting his muscles into knots.

CHAPTER NINETEEN

Wolfe took two of the Mark 19 grenade launchers, carrying them by their tripod mounts. They were bulky, but he used his strength to muscle them level. He walked fast, staying in front of the other volunteers, who were carrying machineguns and nearly endless amounts of ammunition.

"Is this too much?" he asked one of the old veterans. The expression on the man's face was one of pure joy. He was having fun. Too much fun, probably.

"Nah!" He threw one hand down for emphasis before pointing to the ground. "Put one of those right here. We can lob grenades in front of them, into them, or behind them, if need be. This thing will shoot as far as you can see."

The road turned out of sight at two-thirds of a mile. Wolfe had to trust the man since he didn't know. The stubby shells of the short-barreled launcher did not seem like they would travel that far, but the man was confident of the weapon's placement.

The group crossed the road outside the compound and dropped into the ditch. The veterans pointed at regular intervals and ordered that a heavy machinegun he referred to as Ma Deuce be put there. They continued until they were nearly at the bend. The older of the two veterans climbed out of the ditch and described the plan.

Wolfe put the Mark 19 on the ground and listened.

"There were nine trucks, and they were driving single file. That means we have to wait for the last of the nine to clear this corner before we open fire. You cannot let them see you, but you have to count the trucks. Fire up the last truck when it gets right in front of you." The old man mimicked holding the twin handles of the fifty-caliber machinegun and pressing the butterfly lever to fire it. "Spray back and forth through the cab, then the canvas in the back where the troops are after you've shot the engine and stopped the truck."

He pointed back toward the main gate. "And then I'll take out the first truck. You have to keep your guns in the ditch. It'll take two people to lift it over the edge and set it in place. Practice that a few times until you can do it, then start firing in a couple seconds. Any longer than that, and they could drive out of the kill zone."

He fired his make-believe weapon again. "When you've eliminated the threat in front of you, pick the next truck down the line and fire. Watch your line of fire so you aren't shooting through the trucks and into the compound, although there won't be hardly anyone left in there. We'll be out here. If they somehow get out of their trucks, use your rifles to shoot them. We can't let a single soldier escape."

"I'll be at the gate with one other, making like I'm one of the guards they left behind, and my friend here will be right there, ready to deny enemy movement through the use of the grenade launcher. We're going to blow a lot of stuff up, so don't be stingy with ammo. We only get one shot at this. Questions?"

"How do I load this thing?" one of the women asked. The veteran took one of the weapons and placed it in front of the group.

He ran through the steps: raise the top cover, drop the belted ammunition in place, jam the cover down, then cock the weapon. He made the loaders practice it. Many couldn't pull the handle to the rear so he demonstrated the proper jerking technique. Even Wolfe did it, but with his strength, he cocked it easily. "I will be at the gate with you but they will not see me."

The man nodded before clapping his hands. "Everybody get into place and get yourselves ready. It's time to put on your game faces. Practice putting the guns over the berm. Only cock them once. Be ready to fire. There won't be any time to waste. And show no mercy."

Wolfe decided it was best not to mention the Alston brothers. He could scour the bodies later to find what was left of them. He sobered at the thought. Maybe the old vet had been right. This was the battle to end it once and for all.

CHAPTER TWENTY

Jennifer and Buddy ran to meet him on the long walk back to the main gate. He wrestled with the dog briefly before continuing on his way. The other volunteers had fallen back, tired after being up all night. The morning sun had not yet peeked over the horizon, but dawn was bright enough. A blue sky suggested a nice day waited for them.

They could not say the same thing for the soldiers.

Once at the gate, Wolfe sat behind the block that supported the gate arm. He checked to make sure he could see the road and tried to relax. He made sure there was a round in the chamber of his AR-15 and extra magazines readily available. He put two in his pockets and two more on the ground beside him.

Jennifer and Buddy stood next to the entrance and watched him. Bessie made her way to the front gate from inside the compound. She nodded to Wolfe and called for Jennifer to join her inside. "Let's keep getting breakfast ready. These folks will be hungry when this is over."

Wolfe appreciated the confidence, but he did not feel the same way.

The old veteran finally arrived and looked worried. He worked over the grenade launcher to make sure that it would deliver when needed. "I'm not sure, Mister Wolfe."

"You can call me Jim. I never got your name."

The old man laughed. "It's Jim too, but you can call me James if it makes it easier." He sobered and pointed down the road. "With Steve at the far end, we'll put a major hurt on these guys. I'm not sure about anyone else. I figure half of them won't fire a single round, but with these babies," he tapped the barrel of the Mk 19, "we'll be able to stitch grenades the length of the convoy. They won't know what hit them. Trained soldiers would get out of the trucks and attack the ambush, but FEDCOM soldiers don't fall in that category. They've never been challenged. They don't know what it's like."

"Some of them have been challenged," Wolfe replied, his face as hard as leather in a brisk desert wind. "They might not be what you consider real soldiers, but they are mean. Many will die, but the rest will fight, angry and determined. Some might be cowards. Hell, I think most of them are cowards, preying on women and the weak, but that does not mean they will stand there and let us kill them. You and Steve will carry the day. We will clean up the rest."

Bessie had to walk all the way to the gate. "You need to come with me."

"I need to be here for Mister Wolfe," Jennifer replied.

"The last place you need to be is out here," Wolfe said. "Get breakfast ready. As long as no one is shooting, bring us something, will you? That will help keep us sharp."

"Good call. You know all about soldiers and chow. Gotta eat. Need fuel to keep the engine running."

Jennifer thought it might have been a ploy to get her out of the way, but it made sense to her, and she did not want to disrespect the man who had sworn his life to protect her. She had understood what that meant when he'd killed the two guards at the border station where the convoy of soldiers was now going. She nodded and left with Bessie. Buddy wanted to stay outside but joined her when she called to him.

James turned to Wolfe. "You haven't served, but you've had run-ins with FEDCOM. I can tell that you have no love for them."

Wolfe did not answer. He watched the road while tightly gripping his rifle.

"Looks like we got some time to kill. What happened to you after the guvmints tore the world apart?"

The sun finally arrived. "What time is it?" Wolfe asked, avoiding the question.

The old soldier checked his watch. "Looks to be about six. Whaddaya figure? Hour out and an hour back? They don't take it easy on those trucks, and it's about sixty miles."

"If they go all the way. I am worried that we are counting on them to believe it was a prank and not a setup for an ambush."

"They've never been challenged, so they don't know no better," James replied. "It's a good plan, and we are as ready as we'll ever be. This is the best chance we've had in more than two years."

Two riders on bicycles pedaled around the corner, pumping hard. Steve stood up from the ditch and waved to them, yelling something. They waved back and continued toward the front gate.

Wolfe stood and moved into the road.

It was the brother and sister, faces dirty from road dust and muddy sweat.

"They took the bait!" the young man said, excitement raising his voice more than he intended.

Wolfe had told them to stay off the main road and to go home. They had ignored his request for a reason. He wanted to know what it was.

"How many trucks did you see, and how fast were they going?" Wolfe asked.

"Nine, and they were *flying*," the girl exclaimed.

Wolfe and James shared a look.

The boy added, "That was at exactly five-fifteen."

"They were flying." James looked concerned. He turned to Wolfe after doing the math in his head. "That shortens the timeline."

"Thank you both. Anything else you saw as they drove by?"

They shook their heads.

"Go on home, now," he told them. "You put this in motion, and I cannot thank you enough. I do not want to see you get hurt, so you need to go. Get home. Get inside, and keep your heads down." He was too young to be drafted by FEDCOM. Extra hands, but if the volunteers lost this fight, the soldiers would execute every single person they found.

"I know you can, but you served well. You need to go home now. It will not be long before they are back. This fight will be the worst thing you will ever see, so much so that you may never forget it. I cannot be responsible for doing that to you. Go home. Check back after the shooting stops to see who won. If it is us, come back and help clean up. If not, do not show your faces."

Wolfe pointed with his rifle.

The two stood their ground.

"Go on!" James said in his gruff, old-man voice. They finally gave in to the adults and hopped on their bikes to ride the rest of the way home.

"I better make sure Bessie and Jennifer can get out of here

if things go south." Wolfe backed away from the main gate area and then walked slowly. He wanted to run, but if anyone in the ditch was watching, they would get the wrong idea and probably panic.

After he walked through the door, that was when he ran.

CHAPTER TWENTY-ONE

"What's wrong?" Bessie said when Wolfe appeared.

"In case they get past us, I'll need you two to run. Escape out the back gate. I will go there now and break the lock for you. Don't hesitate. Just run."

Jennifer was shaking her head, small chin raised in the air defiantly.

"Promise me!" Wolfe did not have time for being cordial or having a conversation.

"I promise. I'll get her out of here," Bessie stated.

Wolfe nodded and ran out the back door to the back gate. It had a heavy chain across it without a lock. He pulled the chain away and threw it aside, then pushed the roller gate, a section of fence with razor wire on top, to the side, leaving a gap wide enough for a person to go through. There was a wide paved alley and a small stand of trees beyond it. All they had to do was run a hundred yards and disappear.

Wolfe sprinted around the building, slowing to a brisk walk when he came within sight of the front gate. He returned, breathing hard, not from his efforts but from worrying that he had missed something.

James was happy to lean on the barrier as the former guards had. The grenade launcher was behind him, with a clean line of sight down the road. All he had to do was step back, drop, and start firing.

They settled in to wait. After fifteen minutes, Jennifer arrived with two plates. The men took them but hesitated. She had a bag, too. "For the others," she said.

"Make it fast, and stay in the ditch," Wolfe ordered. She ran down the road and disappeared to the side as soon as she could. The big dog ran after her as if it were a game.

Twenty minutes later, she returned empty-handed. She waved as she trotted past. Wolfe watched her all the way into the big building.

"Your daughter is a good one. Raised right. A sparkling gem in this barren world," James said without turning toward Wolfe, who remained seated behind the barricade.

An hour went by, and nothing. Seven in the morning came and went, then seven thirty.

"Something's wrong," Wolfe growled, standing and craning his neck to see the bend in the road. While standing, he could hear the engine screaming toward the red line.

"Here they come," James confirmed. He took a quick look to make sure nothing had gotten in the barrel of his weapon, then gave Wolfe a thumbs-up. Wolfe knelt behind the barrier and looked over the barrel of his weapon, ready to shoot. The first truck appeared, and then a second. They started to slow.

The third truck and then the fourth came into view. James waved friendly-like, as he expected the other gate guard would have. He held his ground.

The fifth truck, and then the sixth. When the first truck slowed, the others started to bunch up.

Perfect, Wolfe thought.

The seventh truck, and then the eighth. The first was getting close. It was not more than a hundred yards away.

"Can't wait," James exclaimed. He stepped backward and tripped, falling on his butt. He scrambled back to the Mk19 and fired into the grill of the first truck. He held the trigger down, and grenade after grenade hit and exploded. The truck bounced and bucked violently before flipping sideways, dumping everyone from the back into the road. They were already dead from the violence of the impact.

James dropped a couple grenades into them for effect. The truck was sideways in the road and blocked their view of the remaining trucks.

Four seconds had passed since the old vet had fired the first round.

In the distance, a fifty cal barked and a truck screeched in metal-tearing agony as Ma Deuce made her deadly call. Steve maintained the weapon's maximum rate of fire, but Wolfe could not see what he was shooting at.

James fired into and through the first truck, hoping to hit anything behind it, then angled up and fired a series of grenades over the column of trucks. He could not see where they landed.

He ran a series of grenades along the shoulder on the right side of the road as he looked at it to stop any soldiers from escaping toward the compound.

Wolfe took off running, staying as close to the fence as he could while James fired sporadically when he thought he could see a target. A second fifty cal opened up, much to Wolfe's relief, but then the worst sound in the world came to him—small arms fire, and too much of it. The underground volunteers were under attack.

CHAPTER TWENTY-TWO

The second truck was on fire, and anyone who had been in the back did not survive the withering attack of grenades fired through the first truck. The third had been stitched by fifty cal but was still mostly intact. The fourth and fifth were getting the full treatment from the ditch. The last three trucks were getting the unbridled attention of the end of the ambush line.

Where was the ninth truck?

The soldiers were staggered around the fourth truck, firing toward the ditch. Two lunged forward and disappeared. They had their backs to Wolfe, and he charged.

Starting at one end, he used the butt of the rifle to break necks. He made it to the third man before they saw him. He rotated the rifle and fired as fast as he could pull the trigger. One soldier panic-fired and another sent rounds into the ground at Wolfe's feet, but Wolfe kept moving. He finished the men and made to turn toward the ditch, but a fifty cal started pounding on the truck.

He veered to the right, back toward the fence, and dove to the ground. His plan seemed more certain now that the volunteers in the ditch had resumed firing. All trace of small arms fire stopped. The fifty cals kept pounding away until someone started yelling. "Cease fire. Cease fire!"

It was Steve.

"Woohoo!" James yelled from the other side.

"Don't shoot me!" Wolfe shouted before standing. "Wolfe, coming out!"

He slung his rifle and held his hands up before he slowly made an appearance on the ditch side of the trucks. Once clear, he hurried toward the ditch, to find the two volunteers positioned where the fourth truck had stopped. They had never gotten their weapon into position to fire. They had died with the machine gun next to their feet in the ditch.

Wolfe looked up and down the ditch. Four machine guns were positioned on the edge of the ditch. Only two had not been put into action. The barrels of two glowed red from the heat. The fourth radiated slightly. It had probably been the last to start firing. Steve had never used his grenade launcher. He had stuck with the heavy machinegun, delivering death at a cyclic rate of fire.

"There were only eight trucks," the old veteran reported.

"It begs the question, where is number nine?" Wolfe said before beginning the grisly task of looking at the dead bodies to confirm the Alstons were among them. He started with the fourth truck, but had seen those soldiers up close. He went to the fifth truck and checked the back. It should be easy enough since the Alstons were not wearing military uniforms.

The soldiers in the last three trucks looked too young to be dead, and none of them were the Alstons or the major.

Wolfe returned to the front of the column, checking the third truck and then the second. The first truck's passengers were scattered across the ground, many burned and shredded. Wolfe could not tell. He studied the bodies as much as he could stomach.

The Alstons had been in the first truck on the way out. It made sense to him that they would be in the first truck on the return trip, but his gut told him the truth. The Alstons and the major were in the ninth truck.

Jennifer appeared. She ran up to him, hitting him with the full force of her twelve-year-old body. She wrapped her arms around his waist and held him tightly. He let her hold him for a while before he squeezed her back. Jennifer was happy he had survived. For the moment, it was the victory they had, but he was afraid for all of them.

The Alston brothers still lived.

CHAPTER TWENTY-THREE

"I'll put someone down on the corner to watch," Steve said, gripping Wolfe's shoulder as a brother in arms. They had fought together, a hard but quick battle. Wolfe nodded.

Steve moved off to take care of it.

But it was too late. The sputtering rumble of the ninth truck reached them before they could get anyone in place. It skidded to a stop as soon as it came around the bend and sat for a second before soldiers started to climb out the back.

"Take cover!" James yelled from near the gate. Steve repeated the order before the sound of small arms fire filled the air. Steve jerked and fell, a red stain spreading across his chest. Wolfe took aim and fired, but he did not hit anything. The fifty cals were across the open area, away from the trucks. Wolfe knew if they were to have a chance, they needed the heavy weapons. The soldiers saw them too.

Wolfe bolted into the opening and sprinted for all he was worth. Thirty yards away, with bullets zinging by, he dove, tucked, hit the bottom of the ditch, and rolled back to his feet. He rushed back to the berm, rotated the fifty cal toward the soldiers and pressed the butterfly trigger with his thumb.

The heavy machinegun started to bounce, and he fought to keep it from falling into the ditch. It appeared that the safest place to be was where Wolfe was aiming. He was spraying bullets high and wide.

He jumped out of the ditch and sat behind the machinegun so he could control it. Two soldiers were manhandling the machinegun Steve had been firing. Wolfe ripped them apart with the power of the fifty caliber rounds.

One of the Alston brothers peeked around the back truck and fired an M16. Wolfe lit into the military vehicle and laced it back and forth, and the truck burst into flames. His machine gun jammed and he threw it aside, then jumped back into the ditch to retrieve his rifle and ran in the direction of the bend in the road.

Wolfe thought he'd seen an Alston running before he was able to accurately fire the machine gun. Looking over the barrel of his rifle, he stood up when he was even with the ninth truck. Over the edge of the ditch, he saw that the machine gun had wrought far more damage than he'd thought it would. Two soldiers were on the far side, confused, walking in circles without their weapons. Two men in civilian clothes were running.

He scrambled out of the ditch and ran after them. Shooting them in the back was not in his plans. This had become too personal.

A dog barked nearby. And again.

Buddy. He had his own beef with the Alstons.

But if the big dog was there...

With the rifle in one hand, Wolfe ran, legs pumping. When he cleared the last truck, he saw her—Jennifer racing after the dog. The Alstons saw their opportunity and turned. Wolfe tried to bring the rifle up, but the girl was in the way. The only thing he could do was keep running to try to get to her before the Alstons did.

The brothers split up, one heading for the girl and one heading wide, slowing down, aiming.

Wolfe dodged at the same time as the rifle cracked. He kept zigzagging to ruin his enemy's aim while continuing in the general direction of the girl. The brother was going to reach her first.

It was a hard decision, but he couldn't face both brothers at once. Wolfe dove to the ground and, lying there, aimed true and sent three rounds into the second Alston. The man looked surprised. The invincible Alston brothers. He toppled over, eyes open, staring at mortality.

Wolfe climbed to his feet and started walking, rifle up, aiming at the Alston who had somehow dodged the dog and was using Jennifer as a shield to hold Buddy at bay.

The Alston tried to shoot around Jennifer, but she was fighting. He could not hold steady. He snapped off a couple rounds, but they weren't even close. He gave up.

"Call the dog off and I'll be on my way," the brother yelled. "I'll hang on to her as an insurance policy, but I'll let her go when I'm out of sight."

"Since when does an Alston keep their word?" Wolfe fired back.

"We said we were coming after you, and here we are!" the brother declared proudly.

"Yes. Here we are. One lying in a pool of his own blood. The major back there, almost cut in half from being on the wrong end of a machinegun. And here you are, counting down the last seconds of your life."

"Big words." The brother shrugged. "I'm taking her with me, but now I'm not going to let her go. She's going to birth the next generation of Alstons."

Jennifer stomped on his booted foot and jerked to get free but didn't make it. The brother back-handed her across the head and pulled her against his body, eyes watching her protector.

Wolfe's blood ran cold. He would rather see Jennifer dead than suffering at the hands of an Alston the way he had described. He could not believe he was considering it. A hard world called for hard times, but that wasn't the man Wolfe could ever be. He brought his rifle up and fired a round over Jennifer's head that parted the Alston brother's hair without touching his skull.

Missed!

The brother flinched and loosened his grip. Jennifer jumped free and grabbed Buddy, swinging the big dog around as she hugged her best friend.

Wolfe fired again. The round ripped through the brother's shoulder, and he dropped his rifle and fell to his knees. He held out his good hand for Wolfe to stop.

"Who died and made you God?" the last remaining Alston brother shouted while wincing in pain.

"I guess civilization did," Wolfe replied. "Someone has to keep the peace and respect natural law. You're a rapist, a murderer, and a thief, and you lied about it all."

"You're already worse than me," the man said from his knees, making no attempt to rise. Wolfe kept the rifle trained on the man's face.

"I have to dispute that, but it does not matter. You can contemplate that while you wait for me in the hellfire where your soul is going."

"We can cut a deal!" the man begged. Buddy growled from nearby, but Jennifer kept him from getting loose.

Wolfe pulled the trigger, sending a 5.56mm ball round through the man's stubble-heavy face. The back of his head exploded and what little brains the last of his line had flew into the greenery beyond. "No. We cannot cut a deal. I have to look at myself in the mirror. And I do not have time to watch my back. Not anymore. I need to get home to Florida, and you have already delayed that far longer than I wanted."

Wolfe stepped away from the body. Jennifer was there in a heartbeat, leaning against him to give him support. The big dog sniffed the dead man before lifting his leg and marking him.

"Come on, let's go get some breakfast," Wolfe told Jennifer, keeping his arm around her as they walked slowly toward the main gate.

CHAPTER TWENTY-FOUR

There were tears as well as cheers when Wolfe walked through the main gate. Six had died, including one of the old veterans. Wolfe stopped to give his condolences to James, his friend.

"No need, Mister Wolfe. He died in battle with the enemy. At our age, we never thought we'd get the chance to do that. In the end, we won, and the people of Ashland are now free. It is what he wanted. It's what we all wanted, and we have you to thank for that."

Wolfe shook the old man's hand, taking care not to crush it.

"I'll take care of everything. We'll gather the weapons that are in good order and burn the bodies. We'll leave the trucks in the road since we don't have anything to move them with."

"Get some breakfast first," Wolfe replied, motioning toward the building. "Unwind, then clean up."

The volunteers from the underground filed past, each saying a kind word or two to Wolfe and Jennifer while Buddy sat next to them, tongue out and panting. It was going to be a warm day.

"What do we do with those two?" James asked, pointing to the soldiers who wandered mindlessly, being prodded along by one of the women volunteers.

"If they have not committed any crimes against these people, they might have a place in the community. They are shell-shocked. They may get over it. They may not. But I do not think they are a threat."

"We'll keep an eye on 'em, Mister Wolfe."

After everyone had walked by, including the soldiers, Wolfe and Jennifer followed. They had already eaten once, but Wolfe was hungry again. He was used to going without, but he was also getting used to Miss Bessie's cooking. They joined the short line that went into the corridor as people rolled past the serving counter.

"Omelet!" someone ordered.

"Take your scrambled eggs and go on!" Bessie yelled back in good humor.

Jennifer pulled free. "Watch him," she said before going through the door into the back of the kitchen and closing it behind her.

"Come on, dog. We'll get ours up front." Buddy started to whine and scratched at the door. Wolfe knelt to look the big beast in the face. "You did everything you could. We took care of them. For hurting you. For threatening Jennifer. For making my life hell. None of us asked for it, but the Alstons gave us grief anyway. They are gone now, Buddy, and we can continue on our way."

Wolfe ruffled the long hair on Buddy's neck and head. "If you are a good boy, you might talk Miss Bessie into breakfast for you, too."

"He is always a good boy!" Jennifer replied from inside the cafeteria.

"If you say so," Wolfe said. "Gemini might have a different idea. He is still short one sandwich."

When Wolfe and Buddy reached the counter, little remained. Only scrapings from the pan that had held the eggs, but Bessie produced a small mound of fried potatoes. Wolfe's mouth started watering. It had been doing that a lot around the older woman. He appreciated anything he did not have to cook himself, and even more when it tasted good.

"And this." She cut a slab of ham in half, giving him half and placing the other on a plate where the rest of the eggs found a home. Wolfe looked at his plate with meat and potatoes. An all-American meal.

"You've already had your eggs," Bessie told him. Jennifer grabbed the plate and hurried around the counter to put it on the floor. Buddy inhaled most of it without chewing and looked up, expecting more.

"He is always hungry," Jennifer explained.

"I know." Bessie helped herself to some potatoes and leaned back with a sigh. "Is it real?"

"No soldiers remain in Ashland."

Bessie glanced at the two men in uniform who had not touched their plates.

"Call them prisoners of war. There are probably two more at the checkpoint out west, but they are sixty miles away. If they start walking, they might make it in a couple days. They are the ones to watch out for, but James has a plan. Ashland will not be unguarded. And chances are, they will not walk all this way. They will rot on that post before they abandon it."

"What about you, Mister Wolfe?" Bessie asked.

"Call me Jim." He closed his eyes as he adjusted his welding goggles. "We will be on our way, probably tonight after we have gotten some rest. It is safer to travel at night."

"Why don't you take one of the FEDCOM vehicles?" Bessie asked.

"I do not want anyone to confuse us with FEDCOM.

They do not have the best reputation among decent people." Wolfe smiled grimly. "But not having to walk the whole way sounds nice."

"Take 160 east, then turn south toward Arkansas. You will avoid the big cities that got hit by the bombs, like Tulsa and Wichita. It should be clear. Then turn south through Louisiana."

Wolfe knew most of the roads from his time as an over-the-road truck driver. Bessie's plan made sense.

"Is FEDCOM anywhere else in Kansas?"

Bessie shook her head slowly. "I wish I knew, but I don't."

"Maybe we will drive a little way before dropping the vehicle by the side of the road and continuing on foot. Driving at night gives me the chance to see them before they see us."

"We want you to stay. Both of you. Welcome for as long as you like."

Wolfe nodded, but he could not. Not as long as he did not know the fate of his Lurleen and little JoJo. "We need to get home. Find out for ourselves if my family survived."

"Gemini is at the boardinghouse." Bessie wiped her hands on her apron. "Finish your breakfast and go get some sleep. We have some work to do here, and then we need to collect everything we promised. We had a deal. You delivered. Now it is our turn to do something for you."

Wolfe ate, leaving a few potatoes and half the ham, which he put down for the big dog. Buddy dug in, making it disappear in seconds. Jennifer picked up both plates and handed them to Bessie.

Jennifer took Wolfe by the hand, called Buddy, and waved to the volunteers at the tables. They leaned heavily, tired beyond measure after a long night and an intense battle, the loss of their own, and the new burden of freedom, yet they started clapping as Wolfe walked out. Stood to see him on his way.

Twenty souls cheered for Jim Wolfe. He was happy to have his goggles. He waved back. Like them, he was bone-tired.

CHAPTER TWENTY-FIVE

Jennifer, Wolfe, and Buddy, the half-wolf, half-German
Shepherd, stood at the entrance to the boardinghouse.
It was dark, but the town's lights were on. Muted cele-
brations were taking place in many places.

"It may not be over," Wolfe told Bessie.

"We know, but we also know we can fight back. We won't
let them beat us down again."

"I hope you are one of many." Wolfe held out his hand,
but Bessie pulled him into a hug instead.

Gemini started the pickup truck he had "liberated" from
the FEDCOM facility. The vehicle rumbled to life and settled
into a smooth idle. Gemini put the two packs and other
supplies behind the driver's seat.

It had been a while since Wolfe last drove, but he looked
forward to getting behind the wheel. His boots were sound,
but he trusted that he would get more chances to walk. He
estimated they had fifteen hundred miles remaining. Shaving
off any of those miles would be a good thing, especially for
Jennifer and Buddy.

"I put a pie between the front seats. Enjoy it. Think of us

as you continue your journey, and most importantly, I hope you find your family. You are a good man, Jim Wolfe."

He nodded, tight-lipped.

"He's my dad," Jennifer said, poking Wolfe in the stomach as she coaxed Buddy into the truck. He jumped in the front and was face-down in the pie before Bessie could stop him.

"In the back seat, dog!" Wolfe was ignored. Once Buddy was done with the pie, Wolfe pushed him out of the front seat. The dog jumped out at Jennifer's urging and climbed into the back, still licking his dog lips clean of red berry filling. Wolfe handed the pie tin out. "At least you get your tin back."

"If I had my spatula..." She shook a fist at the dog. Jennifer hugged the old woman before climbing in and closing the door behind her. She looked around.

"Seatbelt," Wolfe said.

She did not remember riding in a car. He reached across her and pulled the belt over her shoulder and across her lap, clicking it in place. He showed her how to push the button to release it. She tried it a couple of times on her own before smiling with her newfound knowledge.

"Keep that on while we're going. It'll keep you safe."

"Just like you, Mister Wolfe."

He nodded. The car stereo was playing softly, but there were no radio stations. There was a CD in the player. Wolfe ejected it and looked at the label.

Hank Williams.

"Things are looking up, Miss Jennifer," Wolfe said. "I'm about to introduce you to one of the titans of the industry." He pushed the CD back into the player and turned the volume up. He waved as he gave the vehicle a little gas and eased down the road. He made it to the corner, took a left, and pointed the truck's nose to the east. When they cleared the lights, he dimmed the truck's panel and pulled his goggles off. He settled for an even speed of thirty miles an hour.

They had fifteen hundred miles to go. It was a marathon, not a sprint.

Wolfe looked over to find that Jennifer was already asleep. Buddy was snoring in the back seat. Wolfe rested his hand on the young girl, focused his attention on the road ahead, and tried not to think about what they would run into next.

At least it wouldn't be the Alstons.

The End

Nightwalker, Book 5

If you like this book, please leave a review. This is a new series, so the only way I can decide whether to commit more time to it is by getting feedback from you, the readers. Your opinion matters to me. Continue or not? I have only so much time to craft new stories. Help me invest that time wisely. Plus, reviews buoy my spirits and stoke the fires of creativity.

Don't stop now! There's more...

ABOUT THE AUTHOR

Frank Roderus wrote his first story—it was a western—when he was five. It was really awful, as might be expected, but his mother kept that typed and spell-checked short story tucked away until the day she died.

Later, Frank became a newspaper reporter, thinking that books are written by authors which he most assuredly was not. He kept trying to write though, and eventually did it wrong enough to learn how to get it right. That first sale, a young adult novel published by Independence Press, was more than thirty years and a good many books ago.

As a journalist, the Colorado Press Association awarded Frank Roderus their highest award, the Sweepstakes Award, for the best news story of 1980, and the Western Writers of America has twice named Frank recipient of their prestigious Spur Award.

Frank passed away at age 73 in December 2015.

NOTES - CRAIG MARTELLE

WRITTEN JULY 19, 2019

You are still reading! Thank you for continuing all the way to the end.

I'm writing this while I'm in Moscow, Russia, visiting for four days. We used to live here, back when I was in the Marine Corps and stationed at the Embassy. I worked in Arms Control, not with the security guards, but I have to relate a story. At Russia's Tomb of the Unknown Soldier outside Red Square, I ran a Marine reenlistment ceremony about twenty years ago. I was the second-ranking Marine at the Embassy, and I was honored with the duty when the colonel was out of town. We never got permission, so we had to run for it when the police came for us, but I expedited the process, so we were in formation for about ninety seconds. The Russians were a little miffed, but I'm not sure they knew who we were. Maybe some strange flash mob.

But we signed the paperwork and took care of business, keeping the sergeant on board for four more.

I reenlisted a couple times before I was commissioned. I did not have anything as exotic as a Red Square event, though, so I was happy to participate in one that could be memorable.

We walked around Red Square and along Arbat, both old and new yesterday. Lots of memories. I spent two years here. I do speak Russian, but it has been a long time since last I dredged it up from the recesses of my brain. It came back pretty well. I am pleased with how we were able to effortlessly move around the city, getting what we want without having to revert to English.

And no matter where I go, I still write. I guess I never take a vacation from thinking about stories.

Nightwalker started as a project a long, long time ago by Frank Roderus. The first three full stories and half of the fourth were found on his computer after he passed away in 2015. The four titles were picked up by Wolfpack Publishing, but they focus on Westerns, dominating that part of the market. These new books were an exploration by Frank into a post-apocalyptic realm.

Michael Anderle stepped in to license the titles, since we do post-apoc. I went through the books and made only made minor changes before adding an additional 10k words to book 4, trying my best to replicate Frank's style. Since no one had any idea what Frank intended for this series, I tried to divine how it would shake out. I also return a little to my own writing style because the characters are the main players of this story. I think they have remained stalwart features.

Jim Wolfe is a man with a conscience and a sense of personal honor that includes being a gentleman in all things. He is thrown into a world where he might be the only one with those same values. But he has an edge, extreme strength. He has a weakness in that he cannot see in the daylight unless he is wearing his welding goggles. That weakness becomes an advantage because he can see in the dark. Most everything he does is at night.

From the way Frank wrote about Jennifer and Buddy, I think he wanted them to join Wolfe on his journey to Florida, so that's what I did. They are now family, and Wolfe looks after them as his own.

All kinds of adventures await Jim and Jennifer. I already have my plot for Nightwalker 6. I look to write that one, maybe in October. I want to get it to you before the end of 2019. Then Nightwalker 7 and 8 next year.

That's the plan for now. It might change if something takes off. I want to keep all the fans happy, and sometimes that means spreading things out further than I like. But I'll still get to it, because the stories are in there.

Waiting for me to type them in. Back to it, now.

Peace, fellow humans.

Please join my Newsletter (www.craigmartelle.com – please, please, please sign up!), or you can follow me on Facebook since you'll get the same opportunity to pick up the books for only 99 cents on that first day they are published.

If you liked this story, you might like some of my other books. You can join my mailing list by dropping by my website www.craigmartelle.com or if you have any comments, shoot me a note at craig@craigmartelle.com. I am always happy to hear from people who've read my work. I try to answer every email I receive.

If you liked the story, please write a short review for me on Amazon. I greatly appreciate any kind words, even one or two sentences go a long way. The number of reviews an ebook receives greatly improves how well an ebook does on Amazon.

Amazon – www.amazon.com/author/craigmartelle

BookBub – https://www.bookbub.com/authors/craig-martelle

Facebook – www.facebook.com/authorcraigmartelle

My web page – www.craigmartelle.com

That's it—break's over. Back to writing the next book.

BOOKS BY CRAIG MARTELLE

Craig Martelle's other books (listed by series)

Terry Henry Walton Chronicles (co-written with Michael Anderle) – a post-apocalyptic paranormal adventure

Gateway to the Universe (co-written with Justin Sloan & Michael Anderle) – this book transitions the characters from the Terry Henry Walton Chronicles to The Bad Company

The Bad Company (co-written with Michael Anderle) – a military science fiction space opera

Judge, Jury, & Executioner (also available in audio) – a space opera adventure legal thriller

Shadow Vanguard – a Tom Dublin series

Superdreadnought (co-written with Tim Marquitz)– an AI military space opera

Metal Legion (co-written with Caleb Wachter) (coming in audio) – a military space opera

The Free Trader – a young adult science fiction action adventure

Cygnus Space Opera (also available in audio) – A young adult space opera (set in the Free Trader universe)

Darklanding (co-written with Scott Moon) (also available in audio) – a space western

Mystically Engineered (co-written with Valerie Emerson) – Mystics, dragons, & spaceships

End Times Alaska (also available in audio) – a Permuted Press publication – a post-apocalyptic survivalist adventure

Nightwalker (a Frank Roderus series) with Craig Martelle – A post-apocalyptic western adventure

End Days (co-written with E.E. Isherwood) (coming in audio) – a post-apocalyptic adventure

Successful Indie Author – a non-fiction series to help self-published authors

Metamorphosis Alpha – stories from the world's first science fiction RPG

The Expanding Universe – science fiction anthologies

Monster Case Files (co-written with Kathryn Hearst) – A Warner twins mystery adventure

Rick Banik (also available in audio) – Spy & terrorism action adventure

Published exclusively by Craig Martelle, Inc

The Dragon's Call by Angelique Anderson & Craig A. Price, Jr. – an epic fantasy quest

For a complete list of Craig's books, stop by his website – https://craigmartelle.com